COLD AS A DOG

AND OTHER STORIES

Also by Ruth Moore

The Weir

Spoonhandle

Candlemas Bay

Second Growth

Speak to the Winds

The Walk Down Main Street

Voices off the Ocean
Edited by Dean Lunt

For more about Ruth Moore visit:
ruthmooremaine.com

COLD AS A DOG

AND OTHER STORIES

Poems and Ballads from the Coast of Maine

Ruth Moore

ISLANDPORT PRESS

Islandport Press
P.O. Box 10
Yarmouth, Maine 04096
www.islandportpress.com
info@islandportpress.com

First Edition: November 2022
Printed in the United States of America.

ISBN: 978-1-952143-42-7
Library of Congress Control Number: 2022933584

Dean L. Lunt | Editor-in-Chief, Publisher
Piper K. Wilber | Assistant Editor
Emily A. Lunt | Book Designer
Emily Boyer | Cover Designer

Table of Contents

Foreword

by Gary Lawless

For more than fifty years Ruth Moore's ballads have been a part of Maine's oral tradition. Many people have enjoyed tellings of "The Night Charley Tended Weir," as well as Gordon Bok's beautifully sung version of Ruth's "Little River," and Jackson Gillman's wild performances of "The Hangdowns."

High school and college teachers in Maine have recalled that when they recited and discussed Ruth Moore's ballads in their classes, students would come alive, hearing the language of their families, their communities. That spark came from hearing literature that was built from the language that they speak, and realizing that art can be created from their lives, their place on earth.

Ruth Moore's writing keeps alive the language of her particular time and place. Having grown up on an island off the Maine coast, Moore speaks with a true voice, with authority, in a language many recognize as home. In her poem "To A Contemporary Poet," Ruth says, "oh use the simple words / for God's sake do." And in her ballads we hear words that ring just beyond the edge of memory— lollopins, all wovelled up, brim-belay, draggletails, gorming around, spraddled out;

words and phrases from the voices of our grandparents, our ancestors.

This new collection brings together some of Ruth's ballads, poems (even a linked series of sonnets), a little fiction, and a nonfiction memoir which serves as the backstory for her novel, *Speak to the Winds*.

This collection from Islandport Press delivers a great service to readers of Ruth Moore. In her novels, we hear her characters speaking, but in her poems we hear Ruth's voice, speaking directly. She addresses the past, yes, but also the present, and the future. In her poem "The Offshore Islands" she says:

> What follows the time of developers
> No human voice can tell.
> But the silent offshore islands know,
> And they handle their mysteries well.
> They speak with a voice that is all their own,
> And this is what they say:
> That they talk in terms of a billion years
> That their now is not today.
> And the ghosts they brought along with them
> Have never gone away.

In her ballads we meet many characters: Willy, Long-Gone Jones, Skipper McBride, as well as mermaids and gods of the sea. These are stories which seem to rise out of the sea itself, and ask to be read out loud, to be shared and remembered. People, their lives, and their places, eventually become the past, and we are left, as Ruth says in the poem "Remembrance of a Deserted Coastal Village": "To watch the web of water, spinning, spinning, / past these old ruins, lonely and possessed."

In her ballads, her poetry, and her prose, Ruth Moore keeps alive the stories, the language, of her place and time. The epigraph of her first novel, The Weir states: "That was the place that you were homesick for, even when you were there." In this collection, Ruth Moore gives us that place. Welcome Home!

Cold as a Dog

I once see a whale with a gold tooth,
He riz right out of the sea
And opened his mouth in the morning sun,
And showed that tooth to me.

And once I was fishing the Deep Ground,
With nigh six pound of lead,
And I caught a cod as big as a man,
    And he
    Had a man's head.

O there ain't no end to what I'd tell,
Once I was well begun;
Like seeing The Devil rise from the sea
Instead of the rising sun;
Like sea-snakes lashing the moonlit sea,
With their terrible lollopins,
And the little mermaids with their diamond eyes
And split silver fins.

Cold as a Dog

For some have eyes to see strange sights,
And such a one I be,
But I ain't known as a honest man,
   And nobody
   Harks
   To me.

The Offshore Islands

The offshore islands belong to themselves.
They stand in their own sea.
They do not inherit; they leave no heirs.
They are no man's legacy.

Blazing volcanoes, cooled and dead,
Marked nowhere a boundary line.
The rise and fall of oceans left
Not one no trespassing sign.

The money was never minted,
The clutch of its greed so strong
It could honor a deed: TO HAVE AND TO HOLD,
And keep these wild lands long.

The first summer people were Indians.
For some five thousand years
They built up shore-line shell heaps before
They lost to the pioneers.

Cold as a Dog

The white man took what he wanted.
He had privilege, laws, and guns.
He made fast his own boundary lines
And his property went to his sons.

From the west they sailed in Chebacco boats,
And the high-sterned pinkys, Essex-made.
In harbors where water was deep enough
Their schooners carried a coast-wise trade.

The homesteads they made were sturdy,
But those who built near the shores
Had to dig, if they didn't want Indian shells
All over their cellar floors.

Then time slipped by, as inheritance does.
They felt the mainland's pull.
They abandoned their homes to rot away,
And their cemeteries full.

Theirs was the time of history
And written records show
That their hold on the offshore islands began
Less than four hundred years ago.

Now comes the era of real estate,
Of the hundred thousand dollar lots,
Of the condominiums, side by side,
Along the shoreline choicest spots.

What follows the time of developers
No human voice can tell.
But the silent offshore islands know,
And they handle their mysteries well.

They speak with a voice that is all their own,
And this is what they say:
That they talk in terms of a billion years
That their now is not today.
And the ghosts they brought along with them
Have never gone away.

The Night Charley Tended Weir

Charley had a herring-weir
Down to Bailey's Bight
Got up to tend it, in
The middle of the night.

Late October
Midnight black as tar;
Nothing out the window but
A big cold star;

House like a cemetery;
Kitchen fire dead.
"I'm damn good mind," said Charley,
"To go back to bed.

"A man who runs a herring-weir,
Even on the side,
Is nothing but a slave to
The God damned tide."

Cold as a Dog

Well, a man feels meager,
A man feels old,
In pitch-black midnight
Lonesome and cold.

Chills in his stomach like
Forty thousand mice,
And the very buttons on his pants
Little lumps of ice.

Times he gets to feeling
It's no damn use;
So Charley had a pitcherful
In his orange juice.

Then he felt better
Than he had before;
So then he had another pitcherful
To last him to the shore.

Down by the beach-rocks,
Underneath a tree,
Charley saw something
He never thought he'd see;

Sparkling in the lantern light
As he went to pass,
Three big diamonds
In the frosty grass.

"H'm," he said. "Di'monds.
Where'd *they* come from?
I'll pick them up later on,
Always wanted some."

Then he hauled in his dory—
She felt light as air—
And in the dark midnight
Rowed off to tend weir.

Out by the weir-gate
Charley found
An old sea serpent
Swimming round and round.

Head like a washtub;
Whiskers like thatch;
Breath like the flame on
A Portland Star match.

Black in the lantern light,
Up he rose,
A great big barnacle
On the end of his nose;

Looked Charley over,
Surly and cross
"Them fish you've got shut up in there,
Belongs to my boss."

Cold as a Dog

"Fish?" says Charley.
"Fish? In there?
Why, I ain't caught a fish
Since I built the damn weir."

"Well," says the sea serpent,
"Nevertheless,
There's ten thousand bushels
At a rough guess."

Charley moved the lantern,
Gave his oars a pull,
And he saw that the weir was
Brim-belay full.

Fish rising out of water
A trillion at a time,
And the side of each and every one
Was like a silver dime.

"Well," says the sea serpent,
"What you going to do?
They're uncomfortable,
And they don't belong to you;

"So open this contraption
Up and let 'em go.
Come on. Shake the lead out.
The boss says so."

"Does?" says Charley.
"Who in hell is he,
Thinks he can set back
And send word to me?"

Sea serpent swivelled round,
Made a waterspout.
"Keep on, brother,
And you'll find out."

"Why," Charley says, "You're nothing
But a lie so old you're hoary;
So take your dirty whiskers
Off the gunnel of my dory!"

Sea serpent twizzled,
Heaved underneath,
Skun back a set of
Sharp yellow teeth,

Came at Charley
With a gurgly roar,
And Charley let him have it
With the port-side oar,

Right on the noggin;
Hell of a knock,
And the old sea serpent
Sank like a rock.

Cold as a Dog

"So go on back," yells Charley,
"And tell the old jerk,
Not to send a boy
To do a man's work."

Then over by the weir-gate,
Tinkly and clear.
A pretty little voice says,
"Yoo-hoo, Charley, dear!"

"Now, what?" says Charley.
"This ain't funny."
And the same sweet voice says.
"Yoo-hoo, Charley, honey."

And there on a seine-pole,
Right in the weir,
Was a little green mermaid,
Combing out her hair.

"All right," says Charley.
"I see you.
And I know who you come from.
So you git, too!"

He let fly his bailing-scoop,
It landed with a *clunk*,
And when the water settled,
The mermaid, *she* had sunk.

Then the ocean moved behind him,
With a mighty heave and hiss,
And a thundery, rumbly voice remarked,
"I'm Goddamn sick of this!"

And up come an old man,
White from top to toe,
Whiter than a daisy field,
Whiter than the snow;

Carrying a pitchfork
With three tines on it,
Muttering in his whiskers,
And madder than a hornet.

"My sea serpent is so lame
That he can hardly stir,
And my best mermaid,
You've raised a lump on her;

"And you've been pretty sarsy
Calling me a jerk;
So now the Old Man has come
To do a man's work."

"Look," says Charley,
"Why don't you leave me be?
You may be the hoary Old
Man of the Sea,

"But I've got a run of fish here,
Shut up inside,
And if you keep on frigging round
You'll make me lose the tide."

Then the next thing that Charley knew
He was lying on the sand;
The painter of his dory
Was right beside his hand.

He could see across the bay,
Calm and still and wide;
It was full daylight;
And it was high tide.

"H'm," said Charley.
"What am I about?"
The oars weren't wet, so
He hadn't been out.

"Oh," he thought. "Di'monds,
Underneath the tree.
Seems to me I found some.
I better go see."

But he couldn't find any;
Not one gem;
Only three little owl-dungs
With the frost on them.

The Moon & Stars

The November gale, roaring over Popplestone Lighthouse Station, brought more than the usual piles of seaweed and splintered lobster traps. It left a mystery, almost on Jane Foster's doorstep.

The day before, Jane had said to Phyllis Benton over the telephone, "Oh, dear, Phyl! Nothing ever happens out here."

Phyl had just been telling her about the high school basketball game with East Harbor. It had been a drawn battle from start to finish, but the high school had finally won, 21-20. Last year, Jane had been star forward on the high school team; and behind the thin crackle of Phyl's voice on the wire, she could almost hear the thump of feet and the shrill cry of the referee's whistle, as the teams raced up and down the floor.

She sighed a little as she hung up the receiver. She had not minded too much staying home from school this year and keeping house for dad but, she had to admit, life was pretty dull. Popplestone Station was on a rocky islet ten miles out to sea; and the only excitement was when the lighthouse tender called once a month. Sometimes they landed, sometimes not. It depended on how rough the sea was. Last visit, they had had to haul mail and supplies ashore in a breeches-buoy and sail away without coming ashore. The only people on Popplestone were the two assistant keepers, Luke and Jim, and her father, who was head keeper. They were all jolly men and loads of fun, but sometimes they did seem so old! It was just a little unexciting, she felt, when you were fifteen and a really good dancer, and had been voted the most popular girl in school, only last spring. However, it didn't do to think too much about that. She had plenty to do, with her daily duties and keeping up her studying. If only something would happen, though, a little out of the routine!

And then, suddenly, something did. It was almost as if she had rubbed a wishing ring.

She was awakened, that night, by a light outside her bedroom window. Since she could remember, she had been used to the flash of the lighthouse beacon across the walls of her room; but this was different—as if a great flare of lightning had burned, slowly, from somewhere out on the sea. By the time she had shaken the sleep out of her head and had got to the window, it was gone.

The full force of the gale had not yet come. The moon was traveling at a great rate through vast, plunging clouds, and the lighthouse lamp picked out the backs of big grey waves that spat like cats as the wind blew their tops away. Then, as Jane stood, still rubbing her eyes, the light burned again. She saw that it was a signal flare, and made out the mast and rigging of a small sailboat tossing close in upon the rocks.

She remembered running down to the shore and helping Luke and Jim and her father to set up lights; and how they brought out the gun and tried to shoot a line across the breakers. But each time the wind carried it far wrong, and once, when they thought they had struck the boat's rigging, nobody came to make the line fast, and they had to haul it back again, slack and dripping. The signal flare on board died out, and no one lit another, and by what light of the moon there was, not a soul could be seen about the deck.

"Funny," said Luke. "Those first two flares never lit themselves." He picked up the life-line and untied the weight from the end. "Think I might tie this around me and see if I could swim it."

Jane's father shook his head. "Can't be done, Luke. You wouldn't get through the surf."

But Luke went on tying the rope strongly about his wrist. He stood for a moment testing it in his big hands, and began making his way down the ledges.

And then, suddenly, the grandfather of all combers came thundering high up the rocks, and dropped somebody sprawling almost at Luke's feet. He whooped and plunged forward; the foam of the backwash went over him. But the rope was strong and the hands on it steady, and in a moment he staggered back into view carrying something over his shoulder.

Jane, crowding with the others about the flares, saw a slim, red-headed boy of about sixteen, with closed eyes and a very white face. Her heart turned over as she thought he might not be alive; then she saw that he was breathing in great gasps.

"Don't seem to be much hurt," said her father, kneeling beside him. "No broken bones—"

The boy suddenly opened his eyes. "I'm all right," he said, between gasps. "Give me a hand up,"

"Stay where you are," said Mr. Foster. "Luke, you all right? Can you get him up to the house? Jim and I'd better stay here, in case anybody else…" He turned toward the wreck, so close inshore now that they could see the details of her rigging and her valiant plunging mast.

"There's nobody else out there," said the boy. "I was alone aboard."

"You were!" exclaimed Luke, disbelief in his voice. "You sure?"

The boy half raised himself. "I was sleeping aboard alone. I was anchored at—"He stopped. A curious, crafty expression came over his face. "We—we went adrift when the gale struck."

"What boat is she? Where's she from?"

"She's the—" He looked out across the frothing breakers at the boat, and then lay back and closed his eyes. "What do you know about that?" he muttered.

"He's all in." Luke picked him up and started for the house. "He'll think better in the morning."

But Jane, following close behind, saw a strange thing. As the crash came of the boat striking the rocks, the castaway lifted his head from Luke's shoulder and waved his hand—at the wreck, or the sky, or the wind, she could not tell which— and muttered something which sounded to her like "Good-bye, old moon and stars."

In the living room, the boy lay very limp and quiet. He seemed asleep, yet once when Jane came in quietly, she saw him staring around the room with eyes bright as a bird's. Though when she reached his side, his eyes were closed again.

She stood for a moment looking at his curiously-shaped, almost triangular face, and his mop of dark-red hair beginning to curl over his forehead as it dried. He was a nice-looking boy. As she tiptoed back to the kitchen, she wondered where on earth he had come from, and why he had acted so strangely. He was pretending to be asleep, too, but perhaps that was because he was so tired.

She busied herself with hot coffee and sandwiches, knowing how tired and cold the men would be when they came up from the shore.

Things had certainly begun to happen. It would be such fun tomorrow to tell Phyl about it. She could imagine Phyl's excitement! Of course, tomorrow, after the stranger was rested and had told the whole story, it would not seem half so thrilling. But tonight, with the gale thundering and the sea trying to tear the roots out from under Popplestone—What was that? Either she was getting jumpy, or there had been a sound from the living room. Of course! He had decided to wake up and wanted something. Maybe she could ask him some questions, if he were not too tired. Goodness knows, her curiosity was fairly beginning to come out of her ears… She stopped in amazement on the threshold of the room. The couch in front of the fire was empty, and the castaway was gone!

For a moment, Jane stood staring at the empty blankets, before a slight movement on the other side of the table made her turn. There he was—crouched in the corner under the telephone, working furiously at something on the wall.

"What on earth are you doing?" Jane found her voice with a little gasp.

The boy whirled, and she saw for herself what he was doing.

He had a small sewing scissors in his hand and was trying to cut the telephone wire!

There was a little stunned silence. The boy got up and stood looking at her, and her heart turned over with fright, for she was not sure what he meant to do. After all, he was a stranger… no one knew anything about him. What if he— And then her courage came back with a little bump. For his eyes held a sort of hunted desperation, and over his face a shamed red gathered and spread to the roots of his hair.

"Oh!" she exclaimed. "For goodness' sake, don't feel like that! Whatever's wrong, anyway?"

He put the scissors down on the table. "I might tell you I was walking in my sleep," he said slowly. "But I wasn't. I guess it was a case of not thinking, first. I'm not that kind of a guy, really."

"But why should you want to cut the wire? It would have been most awfully serious—the telephone's our only connection with the mainland in case of emergency."

"It is!" He leaned forward quickly. "What—where is this place, anyway?"

"This is Popplestone Island. Didn't you know?"

"Oh-h. Say!" Relief, from something or other, flooded over him. His face lighted up. "I thought, from the direction the wind was blowing—

Jane heard the outer door slam, as her father came into the kitchen. She moved closer. "Who are you, really?" she asked, "and why did you say goodbye to the moon and stars?"

He grinned at her, and she saw, suddenly, that his face was honest and steady—one you could depend on.

"I'm called Reddy," he answered her, "on account of my red top. And as for the rest, why does anybody say goodbye to anything?"

And that, for some days to come, was all the satisfaction her curiosity had. For the strange boy, politely but very steadfastly refused to answer any questions whatever about himself!

"This is a funny way to act, son," said Lighthouse-keeper Foster. They were breakfasting on the morning after the wreck, and the boy, after wishing them a pleasant good morning, was remaining obstinately silent. "I'm not asking you these things out of curiosity. I have to report wrecks and the names of survivors in full."

Reddy's eyes were on his plate, and he made no reply.

"Listen," said Jane, suddenly, her eyes on her father's face. "If you're in trouble, dad and I'll be glad to help you in any way we can." If only daddy would keep his patience!

"Thanks." He looked up. "If you mean that, you could land me on the mainland and say nothing about the whole affair."

Mr. Foster pushed back his chair angrily. "Now, see here. It so happens that there's a law or two, in the lighthouse service, that we have to think about. I don't know what you've been up to—" He eyed the boy keenly— "and I'm sorry if you're in a scrape. You seem like a nice kid. But unless you give me a good, seamanlike account of who you are and where you're from, I'll have to telephone the mainland and have a boat bring over the sheriff to pick you up as a runaway."

"I'm sorry sir. I've told you all I can."

"Very well, then." Mr. Foster got up, and going to the telephone, ground the crank.

Jane looked at Reddy imploringly, and for a moment, he met her eyes squarely. Then he turned away, went out the kitchen door, and closed it firmly behind him.

"Please wait, daddy—" began Jane. But her father already had the sheriff's house at East Harbor on the wire. She waited until she heard him ask to have a tracer for missing boats broadcasts up and down the coast; and then she slipped away quietly out to find the castaway.

Blue Ice and Green Water

Oh, Blue Hill Bay, old Blue Hill Bay
She's a handsome sight to see at any time,
She can sleep in that old sun
Where the winds of summer run,
Shine in winter like a bran-new silver dime.

But don't trust her, boys,
She's wide and she's deep,
Don't mean what she says at all;
Down along her cold ledges
The sea crabs creep
And the kelp it does grow tall,
Boys,
That kelp it sure grows tall.

At four in the morning the lobster boats go,
The seiners come in from the south,
She can shoot back the sun like an I-beam of gold,
And butter won't melt in her mouth.

But check on your sparkplugs
Make sure you've got gas
And gear that won't crumple or crack,
For every three years
She takes a man
And she don't ever give one back,
Not one does she ever give back.

You can call out the Coast Guard
To set off some flares,
And hunt till your eyes drop out blind.
Blue ice and green water is all you can see,
Blue ice and green water Is all you can find.

Blue ice and green water
To the end of the land.

The Ballad of Long-Gone Jones

A hundred thousand miles from land,
A hundred fathom deep,
Sorry Bill and Windyhill
And Salvadore, they sleep.

The cod he et their eyeballs out
These twenty years agone,
And the halibut rolls above the poles
They hung their hammocks on.

But wrinkled like a salted hake
And bearded like a tree,
Lone-Gone Jones come back to land
He never thought he'd see.
  "I only seen horizons,
  For twenty years,"
  Said he.
  "And I will tell you here and now
  Just how
  This come to be."

Cold as a Dog

"I was standing trick with Windyhill
Of a clear night," said he,
"So clear I see a petrel fly
Between the moon and me,

And the ship was sailing soft and sweet,
Like a lady about to sing,
When I looked away to the looward side,
And I see a peculiar thing.

Now I never see such a curious thing
In all my years at sea,
For here come a fog bank blowing in
Against what wind there be.

And before I so much as spit on my thumb
To feel what ailed the breeze,
The vessel slid into that bank of fog
Like a maggot into a cheese.

We gawped at the rigging lights go out
As if they'd been doused in milk,
And Windy's hair crept up on his head
With a sound like rustling silk.

For a minute I breathed them fog-drops in
A-thinking, What can this be?
    I couldn't sing out
    To Windyhill;

He didn't
Sing out
To me.

Then I smelt to the east and I smelt to the west
Like you do when it's thick of fog,
And all of a sudden I smelt green fields
And sun on a cranberry bog;

And out of the mull an island come
Like a ship a-sailing by,
Her bow was made of a granite cliff
A hundred fathom high,
    And the monstrous wave
    From her forefoot
    It riz us to the sky.

We felt the vessel starting up,
And Windy spoke with a croak:
'Missed us, by God!' Said Windyhill,
But that was the last he spoke;

And as I saw that bow-wave roll
Against the milky moon,
The honest thought come to my head
That he had spoke too soon.

We roared straight up through that bank of fog
Into the moonlight white as wine,

Cold as a Dog

I looked around and I see the stars
And the icy cold sky shine.
The comets out of the Milky Way
Come flicking the vessel's spars;
And I see the earth like a rubber ball
Down there amongst the stars;

I see the moon like a big cartwheel
And I touched her as I went by,
If you want to know what the moon feels like,
She feels like a haddock's eye.

Then all of a sudden we hit the top
And we started whirling blind,
And all the rags of all the sails
Went streaming out behind.

Thinks I, When she drops, she'll hit the sea
Like a rock hove into a well,
So I better jump, and so, I jumped,
    And bless
    My dear heart,
    How I
    Fell!

When I see the earth come up to me,
Calm in the moonlit night,
With the ocean as wide as the wide, wide world,
A-waiting for me to light;

And there in the middle of all that sea,
Bone-white, like a damn great tray.
Was the fogbank setting and bubbling,
In a most peculiar way;

And I lit with a monstrous crashing thump
That nigh unshackled me;
But it wasn't the ocean I landed in,
'Twas the top of an ellum tree.

And it come to me like a blast of light
As clear as a boiling-spring,
I'd lit like a bird on that island
That had started the whole damn thing.

Then I heard a terrible moaning sound,
Like a gale in a vessel's spars,
And I see the ship come whirling down
Between the moon and sears.

She struck the sea with scattering crash
And smashed like a china cup,
Nor Sorry Bill nor Windyhill
Nor Salvadore come up.

Well, I peeked through the tree at the island's bow,
And there was a binnacle light,
And a monstrous great wheel and compass-box,
And a critter taking a sight;

And I see one-half
Of a cloven foot;
And I knowed
Who it was,
All right.

Now the voyage I begun that night went on
For twenty year and more;
We sailed all over the seas there be
And never come to shore.

We sailed all over the seas there be,
On mischief and murder bent;
If you hear about ships as never come back,
Why, *I* know where them vessels went.

And how did I come ashore? Says you.
Says you, For here I be.
Well, one night
We had a hell of a storm,
And the island sunk,"
Said he.

March

March comes in crazy.
She can't think what to do.
She draggle-tails old Winter
On behind.
She knows the days of ice
And frost and snow
Are few,
But nonetheless, She can't make up
Her mind.

"Shall I stay Winter?
Or shall I bring Spring?"
She pokes herself
And tries one on
For size.
"Right now I'll show you
What I'm *going* to bring:
Zero. Black frost.
Blizzards. Howling skies.
I'll sneak behind old Winter's doors
And let them slam.

Cold as a Dog

I'm coming in like a lion
So I am.

"You coons go back to bed
And go to sleep.
You earwigs better find
A hole that's warm.
Squirrels, mice and rabbits
Dig in deep,
For I'm stirring up
Tornadium and storm.

"Some of you menfolks took
Storm windows off too soon.
Some of you uncovered
The outdoors water pump
(Ha…ha)
Now you'll see sundogs
And a ring around the moon,
And all the dirty weather signs
I am going to dump.

"This that I'm saying
Is an All-Points-Bulletin.
I'm giving you a warning
And you'd better
Move fast.
Anything you've left outdoors
You'd better rush and

Pull it in,
For there's no way of telling
How long this blast
Will last."

Then March sat down
For a few moments' rest.
She almost went to sleep,
Then woke up with
A jerk.
A monstrous black cloud bank
Was low down in the west,
And it looked as though
This trial-try
Was building up
To work.

She heard the wind let out
A shrill, squawking squall,
As if someone had trod on
A tomcat's tail,
And all of the menfolk
Were hustling by the wall,
Covering up with plastic sheets
Seedling box and pail.

The setting sun looked
Like an egg
That had busted

Cold as a Dog

In the pan.
A handsome rainbow sundog
Was just slipping
Out of sight.
"I've got them all a-going,
Shaking a leg,
They'll finish up what I began
Now I can sleep
All night."

March found a tall tree
And in it she hid,
She went to sleep hearing
A thunderous
Grating roar
Across the offshore ledges
Her answer from the sea.
Then she was too sleepy
To listen any more,
Only to think,
"That roaring sound is me.
I came in like a lion.
so I did."

The owl returned to its thicket
And the moving life of the wood
Went back to tunnels under roots
And the nests beneath
The wall,

Where the flat foundation stone
A silent guardian stood,
And took care of them safely,
Mice, earwigs and all.

March woke up next morning
And slid down the tree.
She did a little
Yawning,
But felt no surprise.
The lovely spring daylight
Was what it ought to be
Not a ripple on the ocean,
Not a cloud in the skies.

The wind smelled of growing,
A sweet passing breeze.
Spring was here
And showing
With no lies or doubt,
And she could hear
The rustle,
Around among the trees,
The hustle and the bustle
As all her friends
Came out.

She wiped the sleep-seeds
Out of her eyes,

Cold as a Dog

Honest as water-weeds
She gave herself
A poke.
"You scatter-brains don't
Recognize
A little early
Spring surprise?
What were you so scared of?
Can't you take a joke?

"You know how I come leaping in
With my cupfuls of weather,
Good or bad
When I begin,
All wovelled up
Together,
So when I told you yesterday
I'd come in like a lamb
You foolish folks
All ran away
Bug down and hid.
I am not irresponsible,
I certainly said, 'lamb.'
So I did.
And here I am.

Crazy old March,
With your weather in a cup.
Don't lie to us—

As if you didn't know.
That green spot
In the garden,
Is a crocus coming up,
Where blew your last thin scarf
Of powdered snow.

Tuxedo Junction: or Where Was That Place?

For a long time I was troubled by cities,
But not now;
And never anymore
Shall the dreams of men, tangible in steel and stone and
    mortar,
Trouble me when I am awake.

What do these do? I asked, leaning out of a window on
    Thirty-ninth Street,
What do these do, that hemlocks and pines or palm trees
    do not?
And why is the breath sucked from my lungs when I look
    at them?

Now I know why.
The names of the poets and painters and last year's best
    sellers
Are printed on the tablets and their likenesses put up in
    the halls of fame;

But who knows what man built this skyscraper?
Who was the architect? Did he have a wife, and was there
    a plaque upon his house,
Saying, HERE MR. BLANK LIVED AND DREAMED HIS DREAM?
Or in any public park is there a concrete-mixer
    set upon a pedestal, with words saying:
THIS WAS THE TOOL HE USED, THIS WAS HIS MACHINE?

The public parks are reserved for the marble generals and
    their trusty horses—
Traveler, and the snow-white mount of
    General Washington.
There the infinite faces of foot-soldiers with rifles
Dream in stone above the cannon and the pyramid-piled
    cannon balls,
And the long lists of names saying who died and who
    came home;
Changed every twenty years for want of room.

When the blueprints are done with they are filed away
    and forgotten.
No one comes back to them and says, "This is a First
    Folio," and draws his breath softly,
And goes away to remember the time he saw a First Folio.

Now I know why.
You read the headlines in the papers,
You listen to the radio,
And you tell me.

The Ballad of The Three Green Waves

No, I ain't got no dorymate.
I goes by myself, alone.
I can't have nobody gorming round
Anything that's my own.

I ain't married and never will.
I come when I likes, and go.
Folks and fussing's all very well
For them as likes um so.

When I puts out to haul my traps
In a good rip-staving sea,
There ain't a soul on the face of the earth
Worrying after me.

Now, there was my brother, years ago,
Got him a wife and kid,
Worried and wore himself plumb out
Being easy in what he did.

Cold as a Dog

We was hauling traps outside one time,
When it come on a howling blow
Cold as a dog and the wind northeast,
Thicker un tar with snow.

Them was the days when we worked with sails,
They warn't no engines then.
I had a peapod and steered with an oar,
But that warn't enough for Hen.

He had a dory rigged up with a mast,
And a mainsail without no jib,
So's he could set in the stern and steer
With a tiller hugged in his rib.

Well, the wind was coming, and Hen
    Shoots up—
One eye on the line of foam—
"Jarp!" he yells, "What in hell'll I do?
I've left my compass home!"

Thinks I to myself, "You goddam fool,
Fixed up like a blooming yacht!
So blasted careful—" I hove him mine.
"Katch!" says I, and he caught.

Hen warn't no good when it come to fog.
Or snow-squalls thicker 'n sin;
But I never see the rampagen yit
I could lose my bearings in.

Down she come and she was a bitch.
I squat on the end of my oar
And I headed into her hard's I could
And let her roar.

I warn't troubled. What'd I care?
I never had no wife.
And as for dying, well, they's them
That's troubled all their life.

"Holler, you damned old slut," says I.
"Holler, and bust your lung.
If i get scared of your going's-on,"
Says I, "May I be hung!"

And I sung all the hymn tunes I ever knowed,
Cause them's the kind you can roar.
I never heard a word I sung,
But my throat got kind of sore.

Then I looks behind and I see three waves,
Following fast as sin,
Each of um reaching his whiskers out
To grab and wrostle me in.

Thinks I to myself, If them ketch me,
(Glory, amen, amen)
They's fish that'll have good feed tonight,
(Revive us again, again).

The first one, he was dark and deep,
And smooth as a coffee cup;
And the next one, he was a slash of foam
Like a kettle boiling up.

But the last one, he was the whole green sea,
And he had a wicked eye,
And slobbery jaws; and "He's the one
As is longing for me," thinks I.

So I spits out over the peapod's stern,
And I turns my back on the sea,
And in a minute, I feels the rise
Of the first one under me.

The first one lifted us up and up,
Soft as a sea of oil,
The next one bit at me going by,
I could see his innards boil.

Six fathom deep in the trough he made,
I looks through the glass-green sea,
Clear as a bell through that last wave,
As was towering over me.

The bare black bottom spread beneath,
For miles and miles around,
And school on school of big sea fish
Looked up without a sound.

Their eyes were buttons off dead men's coats,
Shiny and cold and still;
And the first time ever in all my life
I felt my innards chill.

For whiles I was looking, down come Hen,
Sunk like a chunk of lead
Large as life and as natural,
Only I seen he was dead.

Them big sea fish, they swayed aside,
With a little swirl and a swish,
And then I never see Hen no more
Only the backs of fish;

"Oh, if anything come to me," says Hen,
What would my poor wife *do?*"
And i never cared a hoot in hell,
By gorry, and I come through.

No, when I goes, I goes alone,
Through fire, water and paint,
I ain't got a soul to worry 'bout me,
And I don't care if I ain't.

Advice to Mothers

Mothers, take care what you do to your child
While he is wonderful and young.
Before you write upon him the terrible screed of
    your sorrows
Carve it upon a stone
Which may carry it forever to a grave in the secret earth
But cannot transmit it to its own son.

O mothers, look away from the magic mirror
Which holds you as the widow's arms the maiden!
Your child was not born a solace for your terror,
But for the world's, which he will find more laden
With fear than you, with more than your black sorrow,
If you do not look away from your own yesterday
Into his tomorrow.

Say to him, "Son, it is not a part of duty
To use this power I have over you for harm;
As a child, you have great dignity and beauty;

I see these—in your head upon my arm,
In your body's eagerness, in the love you have for me.
As best I can, I will teach you a man's manners,
But I will not destroy your beauty nor your dignity."

Say, "While you are with me, you shall not be lonely."
Say, many times, "I love you," and "My dear."
Say, "I am not quite the center of the universe; only
Know that whenever you need me, I am here."
O mothers, look around you at the marred children;
Look at the men of business, men of wars.
Look at the senators, Oh God, look at their faces
In the conference rooms where they wrangle over places
In the world's sun, with selfishness and noise.
Cut away sagging jowls, cut away scars
Of greed and insecurity and fright,
And what is left but the faces of little boys
Who cannot find their mothers in the night?

O mothers, send your son away from you
In armor, knowing love is in the world
(He will not understand this while he is little,
But he will remember it when he is grown!)
With the strong tendril of maturity curled
In his man's breast, and behind him no acid shame
From a dishonorable childhood.

Even then you will not be late for your bridge game;
Your homelife will still be nice;
And it may be that your son
Will not be one
Among the hearts of ice
Who paves
The world with graves.

The Ballad of The Mermaid

Hannah, the storm being done, took down her shawl,
And softly, mindful of her husband's snore,
Stole with her basked down the moonlit path,
To see in secret what had washed ashore.

Three days of wind had stripped the trellis bare
Of trumpet-vine; autumn was cold and late.
A bird's nest on the path forlornly seemed
A summer frippery. Quite out of date.

She set a decent rubber on it; then
Easing her body, with rheumatic twinge,
Came to the beach, nor saw, behind, the moon
Made a ribald shadow of her, shawl and fringe.

"It's time to pile the punkins. There'll be frost
Before tomorrow morning, I misdoubt.
If I'd have known how cold a night it is,
I'd have thought twice before a-venturing out."

Cold as a Dog

The sea far out withdrawn, the stricken-beach
Left lonely to the moon, the whispered stir
Of sucker-shells moved something in her mind,
Bits of inspired gossip came to her;

Unthought of ways of circumventing folk;
A penny saved; the sucking pig grown fat;
"That pan I'll solder; and that tennis ball,
Some young one, now, will pay a dime for that."

Sure-footed as a cat, but not so light,
She plodded gravely on to where the beach
Ended in ledges and great rows of foam
The shrieking sea had left. Beyond her reach

She saw a gleaming; grunted; peered; and there
Stark in the moonlight, shining silverly,
Beauty forever kept from mortal eyes
Lay in a pool for Hannah's eyes to see.

She saw bright hair afloat on starlit shell,
A frightened hand that beat the hollowed ledge,
White, blood-stained breasts, a torn and delicate fin,
Scaled, spattered out like jewels at the edge;

And for a moment, while a thin voice cried
A piercing word she could not understand,
Her mind slipped sideways, seemed to spill itself,
And tumble, with her basket, to the sand.

How had the old wives talked, who, dying late,
Had said a bitter name for what must be
In wait beyond unknown, unearthly foam,
To keep their sailor-men so long at sea?

And after all, 'twas *so!* She felt the blood
Move in her veins again; she caught her breath
And crushed the terror rising in her throat.
"You hussy! Scaring decent folks to death!"

She stooped and peered, remembering her God.
"You! With your finny tail and yaller hair!
And not a rag to hide you! How'd *I* be
Flat in a puddle, with my bosom bare?"

There was one thing for decent folks to do,
When devil's spawn like this should drift ashore.
"It's half a fish; and I've kilt fish before."

The clasp-knife from her pocket… then, she chilled,
For as she leaned above the white and gold
And shuddering thing, it watched her, in its eyes
Something as veiled as starlight, and as cold.

No, it was not a fish. She struck and fled.
Clumping across the rocks and up the hill,
Leaving her knife to glisten by the pool,
Her basket for the rising tide to fill.

The Mountain of Snow

As when a little snow, tumbled about
Will make a mountain.
    —W. SHAKESPEARE

I

New England, in my blood and in my bone,
Recall to me my flinty heritage—
Daisy and everlasting, saxifrage,
The slow, reluctant blooming out of stone.
Tough land, recall my toughness of a knot
In hickory wood; the root the boulder bent;
For I unlearn the stubborn words you taught:
Whose breast the sea strokes lies indifferent.
Recall the icy eyes of gull and gannet,
Wingbones and devil's aprons, eels and caves,
For, oh, my fathers in their capes of granite
Are turning, turning, turning in their graves,
That I should be so tamed, caught unawares,
Pliant and passionate. A child of theirs!

II

I do not think, my dear, that spring returning
With wild wet winds to blow its blooms away,
Ever again will set the blind blood burning,
As once it did, in springs before today.
Not spring nor fall, nor any changing season,
Nor petal blown, nor river in its flood,
Nor Beauty's self could be sufficient reason
For this upsurging clamor of the blood.

Therefore, be gentle with me; love me never
So much as now, who in your hands have laid
All lovely things to keep for me forever,
That all the springtimes of my years have made;
Perilously keeping for myself alone
The fearful flame, consuming flesh and bone.

III

This is not new; it is only new to you.
The strength within it soon will make it old.
The human syndrome, steeled in dust, foretold,
Needs only flesh to show what it can do.
See how it flowers there along the nerve,
The candelabra-branching ice and fire,
Path of a lover's fingers, in desire
And tenderness, to trace a body's curve.

No. It was older than primeval cloud,
When the first tiger sprang, the first wound bled;
Therefore, be not ashamed nor over-proud
That ancient custom cradles you to bed,
Heavy as time, strong as a lover's kiss;
But not in tenderness nor love; not this.

IV

I think you do not love me; but be kind
Awhile tonight, and do not tell me so.
Let me stay here and watch the firelight find
The dark foam of your hair before I go.
So quietly the shadows touch your hands,
So frail a spell the falling embers weave.
This is a silence that one understands
How not to break, but dare not quite believe.

Oh, I perceive how all the pitiful rest
Of love is dead and done with; but the strong
Dark tentacle of beauty in my breast
Irrevocably curled, must last as long
As I shall live to keep a small, sublime
Deluded ghost from creeping out of time.

V

The rocks will never miss you, nor the sky.
The sea will be unchanging, oh, my dear;
Tomorrow by this water, only I
Of all things else shall know you are not here.
There to the sea tomorrow's boats will go,
Tomorrow's petrel cut his windy track
Across the cloud-rim; only I shall know
That you are gone and are not coming back.
Somewhere in time, remote beyond belief,
Compassionate summer leased to you and me
A sheaf of days as beautiful and brief
As bubbles, rising, breaking, in the sea.
Remember them for me and help me bear
Pitiless water and impassive air.

VI

The small brown birds are going now; the oak
Lets down his leaves, and frosty fields are bare.
The days of summer, they were less than smoke,
Less than a flight of sparrows in the air.
Light as the bird's wing, softer than her breast,
First snow, for ground the ice has rent apart;
O lovely snow, fill up the ruined nest.
You cannot heal disaster in my heart.

Oh, flake by flake, creep up the bending bough,
And cradle deep the melancholy leaf;
No one but I remembers summer now,
Scattered in time and lost beyond belief.
Kindness on stone, on seed and stubble row,
But not upon my heart, O lovely snow.

VII

Wherefore was I by you a changeling made,
Who tore me helpless out of flesh and bone,
And in my heart as in a cradle laid
A creature unfamiliar and unknown?
That was not I, tormented by a face,
Beset, by fear beat back, and wholly sad
For I was one who loved you with the grace
That long ago a sunny childhood had.

See now: his wings are scattered to the north,
His body flung asunder in the west;
Your child become a goblin, going forth,
Leaves fierce and bloody claw-marks on the breast
That harbored him for enemy or friend.
Wherefore was this? To what ungentle end?

VIII

Wake not to life, O dreamer, for your eyes
See now the compass-point where quest is ending;
Love is a falling star across your skies,
You touch no hand, you do not need befriending.
By this, your dream, you are remote and far,
Wake not from sleep, you do behold the dream;
Forgotten be this life, this falling star,
This reed of sorrow standing by its stream.
Not now the wind, not now the water leaping
To ebb or flow, nor cricket left awake,
Nor any frightened word nor sound of weeping
Can turn you homeward from the path you take.
O hands untaught, that touched but could not break
The crystal box where ecstasy lay sleeping!

IX—1960

If I should see you, if you were the same,
With the face you had, and summer, and that hair,
I would not know you, would not know your name.
You might cross my field like water or like air,
Or spray blown inland from some tall waves wing,
As once you did, when I was watching where
Your footprints vanished by the moss-grown spring.

Why, I might think, what person walks this way
Along this path, leaving one footprint more?
Someone I knew, perhaps, another day?
Not you, but Time, went out and shut the door.
I would not wonder long, nor mark the spot,
Seeing you there unchanged, as I am not.

Skipper McBride

Down on the clamflats
Of Burnt Point Cove
The hull of an old vessel
Lies rotted away.
There's not much left of her—
Some limp, slimy slats,
That the tide runs over
Every day.

But you can see her ghost
If you know how to guess.
You can trace the outline
Of a long, shallow dip,
Covered half with mussel beds
And mud-cove mess,
Where lie the last leftover signs
Of a centuries-dead ship.

She was no clipper
On the China run.
She was a working coaster
Plugging up and down,
With cargoes of everything
Under the sun,
Hauling back supplies and goods
In a ship-building town.

She might be a mystery
At one with mud and silt,
After two hundred years
Of Time and creeping tide;
But she left behind her history
And the way she was built,
Written down by her builder,
Skipper McBride.

Papers thin and tattered
In an old sea chest
Tell she was the *Mary Anne*
Named for Skip's wife.
List of his hand-picked lumber—
He used what woods were best
To build a vessel tough enough
To last a man's life.

Skip didn't buy lumber.
His woodlot was the reason.
First, he cut down and sawed up
His white oak trees,
For white oak, air-dried,
Might take a year to season.
He had time then to ransack swamps
For hackmatack knees.

White pine masts, two sticks
Sized and dressed,
Smooth as the skin
On Mary Anne's back.
Yellow birch for underwater work
Always the best,
That never would rot,
That no jolt could crack.

Skip wrote about a tree, just right
For what he needed,
But under it he found
Hidden in the puckerbrush
An old campsite,
With a lot of Indian arrowheads
Scattered on the ground.

"Signs of an Injun tribe
Drove off and gone.
Let the undergrowth have it
Keep it where it be."
He walked out around it
And then moved on.
"Be damned if I'll use that one.
It ain't a lucky tree."

He carried his own lucky piece,
A gray-dark fossil stone.
The sailor he bought it from
Didn't want to let it go.
Said it meant long sailing
For any man to own.
The little critter in it lived
A million years ago.

Skip wrote about the sailor,
"Likely he lied,
So's he could put his price up
Make me think 'twas right.
But that talk about a million years
Kind of stirred me up inside.
I asked him what the critter was,
He said, 'An ammonite.'

"I asked him where he come from,
He said he was a Greek.
Damn furriner or nothin,
I paid his price in gold,
For that little curled up critter
Done everything but speak,
Said, good luck and long life, and
Old, old, old."

Somewhere offshore
In the tricky Gulf of Maine,
Buried deep or water-worn,
However drowned men go,
Are the bones of Skip McBride
Lost in the hurricane,
Called, in the records then,
The century's worst blow.

It smashed up the *Mary Anne*,
Left her a wreck,
Drove her toward the coastline
Before the mighty blast.
Skip and two sailors washed off her deck,
Trying to cut the rigging
From a floating mast.

Cold as a Dog

Two weeks later,
The mate and three men,
Sailed her home on jury-rig,
A hope and a prayer.
She was too racked out
To go to sea again,
They grounded her on Burnt Point flats
And left her there.

They brought ashore her logbook,
Along with Skip's chest,
It turned up in someone's attic
Some fifty years ago.
Skip's last entry was,
"The weather's turning west.
Come on, you goddamned ammonite,
It's time for you to show."

The mate wrote up the logbook,
A few short notes
That told about the hurricane
And how Skip died;
About sailing home
With their hearts in their throats,
And the vessel half-sinking
On each change of wind and tide.

Skip McBride's lucky piece
That told him what would be,
Doesn't speak of luck now in tomorrows
Unknown.
Says only, lost, forgotten, gone in the sea—
The little curled up critter
In its nest of dark stone.

July

Under the summer sky in peaceful midnight,
In the face of the full moon,
Before the turn of the tide,
Seals, dogfish, pollock, mackerel, all sea-hunters of prey,
Drove a school of brit into the shallows of the cove.

The little fish, frantic, in terror,
Fled, crazed, into the only way they could go.
They plunged headlong to shore, died in windrows,
    gasping, on the beach.

Then,
Out of ledge-crevices, holes in sand,
Out of the green-black sea-bottom woven with
    tide-sucked matted weed,
Countless crabs came, scrambling sideways to the feast.
Claws clutching, mouths gobbling,
They made no sound.
Except for a slight commotion of spray as they crossed
    the edge of water to the sand,

Cold as a Dog

They were silent;
But their wet backs returned bright sparkles to the moon,
And the beach looked as though invaded
By a colony of undersea black stones,
Which had somehow come alive and were moving there.

The tide turned, gray-green, ice-cold.
In the light of morning,
The beach peas rustled in the small breeze that
    comes with dawn.
Trees on the bank quiet, drift still, slight ripple on
    the water.
Land weeds in the clearing flattened with dew.

The clean and empty sand lies under a peaceful sky.

The Ballad of Willy

Down by the sand beach,
Looking for an oar,
I met my brother Willy
Wading in to shore.

"You're wet, Willy,
Rockweed in your hair,
Sand in your pockets.
What's it doing there?"

Willy said, knocking
Clamflats off his shoe,
"I've just come back from being drowned,
If it's anything to you."

"Well, of course it ain't really,"
I said. "Hell!"
But the fact is, Willy,
You don't look well."

Cold as a Dog

I thought my brother Willy
Was drunker than a skunk;
So I says, careful.
"You been on a drunk?"

Willy looked ugly.
Then he says, "Yes!
Half-seas-over
Would cover it, I guess."

"Come home, Willy.
Come and get dry."
But Willy looked seaward,
He hove a long sigh.

"I come down from Cargill's bar,
Last night," said he,
"A-thinking of what lady
Would ever marry me.

"I have had from many
Many a caress;
From Moll and Poll and Mary,
Margaret and Tess;

"From Sue and Jo and Helen,
Annie, Alma, Em—"
"Yes," I says, "Willy,
I know about them."

"I've always thought," says Willy,
"That I was pretty clever;
Out here last night the moon shore bright,
It looked like forever.

"The waves was running up the sand
In little fins of foam,
I thought I'll walk the beach a while.
And then I will go home.

"But as I walked I saw out there
What seemed to be a head;
A head and shoulders floating.
It was right out there," he said.

I see his finger pointing,
His hand all bloodless and white;
A-wrinkled up and parboiled,
Like it had soaked all night.

"Was someone drowned, Willy?
What was it that you spied?
Whose body was it drifting in
The cold night tide?"

"It wasn't no one's body,"
Willy said to me.
"It was the damndest prettiest girl,
I ever hope to see,

Cold as a Dog

"A-floating down the moonpath,
All ringed around with foam,
And not a stitch of clothing on
As if she was to home.

"And while I watched, she waved her hand
And turned herself about,
Says, 'If you want me, you've got to come in,
For I ain't going to come out.'"

"Willy!" I cried. "You're crazy!"
And Willy looked at me.
"I put one foot down off the beach
Into that white foam," said he.

"The first foot I put in the sea,
I felt a cold wind blow;
And the next foot I put in the sea,
I knew I was going to go;

"And when I put my body in,
I saw the moonpath wide
Break to a million diamonds
That tinkled down the tide;

And then I saw her swirl and dive;
Her bright and gleaming head
Was lost in foam and moonshine,
And I think she laughed," he said.

"Willy!" I said. "Willy!"
And Willy looked at me.
"I've swum all night. I've drowned," he said.
"I've vanished in the sea.

"I've see a hundred thousand wrecks.
I've see the pirate's gold.
I've see a million dead men's bones.
Above all, I've been sold."

"Didn't you see the girl?" I says,
"Not anywheres, all night?
For that ain't like you, Willy."
"All right," he says. "All right.

"I've see too many women,
The tall, the thin, the fat.
She had a fish's fins and tail,"
He said, "And who wants that?"

He shook the sand out of his shoes,
The rockweed off his head
"I'm done and done forever.
The foam's my home," he said.

   "Willy!" I said, and "Willy!
   Like you said,
   Are you dead?"

Rocks

The rocks of the earth are its history.
Dinosaur tracks they hold,
They tell what's known of who got here first,
They say how old is old.

Fossil shells on mountain sides
Mark there the depth of seas
That rose and fell with the changing tides
Of numberless centuries.

Creatures came, but not to stay.
Diplodocus lies in his deep.
Time-tried and tossed away
The ammonides sleep.

But not the same are the fossils found
In the Age of Inquisitive Man,
For the tallest mountains wore down to the ground
Three times and are rising again.

Cold as a Dog

Who can write on Time's dust
The secret ebb and flow
Of what roared over the earth's crust
Billions of years ago?

Fierce fires still rage on earth, and within
Rocks shift and fissures crack.
What difference now to who started in
And never did come back?

For the home of Man is already rock,
While his triumphs are shouted and sung,
Whatever volcano or earthquake shock
Tell him how young is young.

The rocks of the earth hold secrets,
Weathered, battered, brown.
Yet a pebble found in a wayside ditch
Might be cut for a king's crown;
And a certain beach-rock, tossed by the tides,
Holds a shimmer all its own.
It takes a polish of silent dark,
As if a black moon shone.

The lapidary who cuts a gem,
Slices his agates thin.
With professional care he handles them,
Finds out what lies within.

For the outside crust of an agate stone
Looks dingy—of little worth.
But inside, when shaped and polished, are some
Of the loveliest colors on earth.

Design is there—mathematical—
A scientist wouldn't be fooled
Over what happened inside a rock
When the gases stiffened and cooled.
But sometimes a difference creeps in,
As the lapidaries know,
When polish shows up a landscape of trees,
With a background of snow.

Or a perfect scene of a big white owl
Sitting poised on the limb of a tree.
What of scientific logic then?
For how could this *happen* to be?

Does some hidden consciousness live in rocks,
Who pokes fun at the human race,
And leaves a portrait for someone to find
Of the devil in hell with flames at his back
And a horrible monkey face?

The lapidary who found this scene
Is thinking, wondering, still.
But nobody has an answer to this,
And I don't think anyone will.

Helen the Princess

Helen the Princess when she was young
Knew wild blossoms and palace flowers,
Watched the silver swans as they swung
Around the foot of the castle towers.

She dreamed no dream of a far-off town
Or topless turrets tumbling down.
Helen the Princess strolled among trees,
And saw bright sun on the wings of bees.

East wind, west wind, spring and fall,
Brought strange ships to the shores of Greece.
Minstrels sang in the castle hall
Salty songs of the golden fleece.

In the market-places where goods were sold
Travelers rattled their rings of gold,
And the castles looked down past sheets of foam
At the galleys of Troy returning home.

Cold as a Dog

Wild in the sky the trumpets pealed
Calling the clans from near and far—
Agamemnon, his mighty shield,
Menelaus, his horse of war,

And the great ships heeled to the thundering wind
With vengeance fast to the banners pinned,
For Helen who smelled of palace flowers,
And watched the swans from the castle towers.

The Ballad of Tryphosa's Husband

He wasn't old and his health was good;
He hadn't no call to go and get queer.
They couldn't have been a better place
For him to be than right out here.

His folks were fishermen, born and bred,
And it never seemed so hard to me
That a man who was all but born in a boat
Should make his living out of the sea;

But every winter when work was slack,
And he ought to been fixing his traps and boat,
He'd set with a seed-book under his nose,
Till I could have jumped right down his throat.

And before the frost was out in the spring,
He'd be digging, down on his knees.
"Ike," I'd say, "It's a fool thing.
You can't grow nothing on rocks like these.

Cold as a Dog

"Even the trees is spraddled out,
cause their roots hit rock and won't go down;
And there ain't much use in garden-truck
Where goosegrass even in June goes brown."

He never give no heed to me.
He was sot in his ways as a hen.
God never meant this place to grow,
And so I told him, over'n again.

But every spring for twenty years,
He dug like he had a kind of craze;
Why, the money he spent on seeds and stuff
Would have kept him in oilpants all his days.

Last year, he got him some good black earth,
Dug up from a farm in on the land,
And he like to of lugged himself to death,
Spreading it onto the rocks by hand.

And all his seeds come up and growed
Green as stuff you'd raise in a can.
Ike was as proud as a pint of milk.
I never see such a change in a man.

I done my darndest. "Ike," I says.
"Weather's a-brewing, and don't you forget.
We'll have a tempest before we're through.
We ain't had a season without one, yet."

But he was a-stepping clean off ground,
And he never could see beyond his nose.
"I've got it licked this year," he says,
"Under the rock the roots grows."

It come in August. The sun rose red
As a kilt pig for a couple days;
And the gulls flew up and made a touse
And took for land; and, "There!" I says.

We ain't had a storm like that for years;
It's a wonder I'm here to tell the tale;
For I thought that the lighthouse was pounding down
The sea made so, and it blew such a gale.

I went to bed, but I never slept;
Four windows blew in in the eastern rooms,
And in the morning, the rocks was swept
Like the angels of God had been there with brooms.

Ike, he opened the kitchen door,
And stood there mumbling under his breath.
"Look," I says. "They's mess enough,
Without you acting like we'd had death.

"Over and over again, I've said
That it won't grow, that it ain't God's will—"
Why, he spun around like a crazy man.
"God Almighty!" he says. "Keep still!"

"You and God," he says, "is done.
I've stood this 'rangueing till I'm a wreck.
Blast you! Blast God! And blast this sea!
Shut up, or I'll break your goddam neck!"

Then he scrabbled his seeds in an old tin pail,
With nary another word to me;
And I s'posed he was going out, like he did,
To heave rocks and cuss at the sea;

So I says. "If you're going out in this,
You better put on your hat and coat."
But he slammed the door. And the next I knew,
I heard the engine start in his boat.

Well, my heart come up! I run upstairs
And pointed the spyglass over the trees,
And there was the boat right off the land,
'Twas horrid, the way he clumb them seas.

The water was rolling over the bow,
And there stood Ike, his pail in his hand,
Right in the face and eyes of God,
Sowing seeds like you'd do on land.

I won't forget till my dying day,
Till they lay me out in my winding-sheet,
Ike, a-planting seeds in the bay.
With his boat a-sinking under his feet.

I figure to go in shore this fall,
It's kind of lonesome, living alone.
I could have felt he was nearer by,
If he was buried under a stone.

But my brother's died and left me a farm,
The letter said there was hens and a cow;
And I can raise garden-truck to sell;
I guess I'll manage to live, somehow.

The Tired Apple Tree

Two neighbors fought a war, year in, year out,
Over who should have the apples from a tree
That marked their boundary line, or just about.
Neither knew, really, where that line should be,
But each believed with spirit, heart and soul
The tree was hers, and both were set like stone.
Whoever got there first, with pail and pole
Was getting apples legally her own.

As time went on, things went from bad to worse.
One lady got an eye as black as coal,
The other, mortally hurt, screamed out a curse,
"Murder! You tried to kill me with that pole!"
She dropped her own pole, grabbed her apple-pail,
And slammed her staggering neighbor on the head.
And the last blows that followed did not fail
To leave one dying and the other dead.

So there they lay. No one had given in,
Even when both were voiceless on the ground.
Whoever got her breath back first would win
Were their last thoughts, in this, the final round.

II

Then silence fell in the tree's shade,
As if the sun and the sky and the air
Had found the place where silence was made,
And under great wings had flown it from there.
No songbirds sang, no bees hummed the clover.
No sign of inquisitive circling crows.
Till a small brown cow came stepping over,
With a sprig of weed across her nose.
She said, "Hi, tree," and stood waiting there
Looking up at the laden boughs.
"I see you've got some apples to spare.
Seems they've left some, this year, for us cows."

Then a voice spoke out like an icy wind
Blowing over a frozen sea.
The leaves shuddered, loosened and thinned,
But not an apple fell from the tree.

"Each year I work a miracle, alone,
Send up my sap to break bleak winter's power,
Mother my boughs and call them all my own,
And on each new-born twig I place a flower.

I use the sun, the generous rain, the air,
Throughout the season my beautiful children grow.
Then my boughs are smashed and twisted, and there…
    there,
Chaos and bloody ruin lie below.

"My roots shrivel, my heart breaks,
At the evil curses, the blows and grapples,
What one of them snatches, the other takes.
You cannot comfort me with love,
And I am sick of apples."

"Don't feel like that," the brown cow said,
"It's not your apples that's to blame.
Now that them two old slumbags is dead,
Things'll never be the same.
Winter's coming with clean white snow
That'll bury this mess in a single day
Let your children go where they need to go,
You've still got your springtime debt to pay."

"I have no springtime debt," said the tree.
"I am leaving my life. I am wilting now.
There is nothing left. Nothing cherishes me."
"Me and my sisters do," said the cow.
"And one thing you don't appreciate,
Though when you're rested, you'll know it well.
Them two creeps killed each other's hate.
It's gone. It's frying with them in hell."

"Gone it may be," the old tree said.
"But hate lives in hell, it comes and goes,
It may spare an hour to bury its dead,
Then how many days of peace? Who knows?
How long stays the gift of the quiet nights,
When summer stars drift over the hill,
When the wheatfield glitters with firefly lights,
And the tick and the tock of Time is still,
Before the wind brings the rotten smell
Of old blood leaked from the centuries?
Hate is stirring again in hell,
The word comes in on every breeze.

"So my children shall stay on my shattered bier
While winter freezes and spring brings rot.
There shall be no leaves nor blossoms here.
Nothing shall grow on this cursed spot.
My message I'll send through air and ground,
To carry my word to my kin, wherever
An apple tree in the world can be found,
Saying, 'Leave this place and be gone forever!
Nowhere on earth will your boughs be green,
Nor apple blossoms again be seen.' "

The brown cow gave a small choked cry.
She whispered, "Oh, no," then turned and fled
Back to the pasture field close by
Where her friends and sisters peacefully fed;
Where the pedigreed bull brought them all around

And led them close to the apple tree;
But to their pleading she made no sound.
A tower of icy cold was she.

III

That night in barnyards all over town
The stock went crazy, broke loose and ran.
They stopped the traffic, charged up and down,
Smashed what they could reach of the things of man.
The pedigreed bull roared his rage to the sky,
Like a tropical storm his thunder rolled.
His ladies performed disasters untold.
They demolished the fish market, passing by.

The townsfolk fled to what they could find;
Some even climbed the trees in the wood,
And the minister cried, "All hate is blind!
To where on earth has vanished our good?"

Then State troopers came and Police with guns,
The sound of gunfire filled the air,
And that was the last, as the story runs,
The battle for justice ended there.

IV

The pedigreed bull came limping over.
On the frozen tree trunk he leaned his head.
"The little brown cow will eat no more clover.
They shot her last night and she is dead.
They are killing the wounded cows today -
The useless ones whose milk has gone sour.
We willingly pay for the glorious hour
When we fought to show you our need of you
Because we love you, us cattle do."

He shivered and raised his battered head.
"They were always too much for us," he said.
The noble blast of his voice was hoarse,
The pride of his footsteps humble and slow,
The way of his going, the shambling course
Of a beaten beast.
The tree let him go.

V

All day the noise of the killings went
Up from the barns of the outraged town,
Over the sounds of quiet lament
That dwindled and ceased as the sun went down.

Silence spread on the falling night,
The chill of autumn blew in on the breeze.
The tree stood alone. Then a growing light
Came from the east, crept over the trees.
Shadows moved as the round, full moon
Shook off the earth and bloomed in the sky,
And the tree watched till she saw, too soon,
The silhouettes of her children lie,
The last apples ever to be.

"Abandoned to rot by a mother's hate,"
Said a cool voice that dropped from the sky.
"Hate is using you now to demonstrate
The power it has, just by passing by.

"I am the moon. I travel alone.
I sail here forever, now, as I must.
My face is winter, my heart is stone,
A dead planet of cold and dust.

"I have no feeling. I do not care
Where my light falls, on seas or shores.
What I was, is my own affair,
But you might guess that it could be yours.

"I am older and colder than you by far,
When I think of the sun, I find much good,
But your earth I see like a falling star,
Or a victim lost in a poisoned wood.

"My orbit is lonely, but this is my place,
Where I look down on you from above.
Over me is the safety of endless space
And I need no part of friendship or love.

"But your earth has plenty of both to give
For goodness and grace could be yours alone
If the evil cloud let your people live,
Not wrangle to death over some small bone.

"I am the moon. I have watched hate's grins
For centuries, seeing what it can do.
It never falters, it always wins.
It has come back. It is now in you.

"And I ask you, who will defend you now
With your outposts falling one by one?
You mourn the loss of a small brown cow
Whose love was needed and now is done."

In a wandering cloud the moon hid,
But showed as she traveled her ageless round,
The tree felt no change. Her apples did.
They twisted and shook and strained for the ground.
Those in the shadow were dim and cold,
But each in the moonlight glowed like a gem
Painted in stripes of silver and gold.
They seemed warm on the boughs. There was life in them.
And their voices called out in gusts of laughter.

"We may go late or we may go soon.
We may roost up here to some wild hereafter.
But who listens now to the foolish old moon?
Poking around in the sky up there,
From cloud to cloud, taking a peek,
Letting its notions out on the air,
To drop down on us, the lying old sneak.

"It's none of its business what we do.
We have no debt, and we may be few.
We are young, we are strong. Let anyone know
That we won't be told which way to go.
Apples shall be while the river runs,
While the rain falls cool on sweetened air.
We will blossom over the sound of guns.
If blood flows again, we will still be there.
So wait, sad tree, for comfort when
Your summer-time comes back again."

September

Work gravely in your garden,
Charles, your child
Beside you, tawny-headed
In the sun,
Waiting for windless dusk
To burn the piled
Old autumn leaves, before
Your work is done.

You watched the garden bloom
In the summer heat,
Weeded and hoed, gathered
In morning light.
Now the rubbish is cleared away
And smoky and sweet
The flower of your fire
Will blossom against the night.

Cold as a Dog

The seed will be here, The stem and the leaf—all here
The spirit to smoke
For the winds of the sky to keep.
While a man goes home
From his work in the fall
Of the year,
To his house and his bed
And the peace of
His winter sleep.

Little River

Little River lighted-whistle
Cry no more.
Sleepy sound from the breakers calling me
Back to shore.
    Whistle it soft to the silver river,
    Whistle it loud to the drumming sea.
    Whistle it low to the moon and morning.
    Not to me. Never to me.

For I'm swinging high in another country
Swinging low,
Playing it cool and the dolphins follow me
Where I go.
    Whistle it loud to the flood tide making.
    Whistle it soft to the wheeling sun,
    Whistle it wild to my girl's heart breaking,
    She'll remember, she was the one.

Spring comes warm over Little River,
Storms come black.
I was headed home when the Indian Giver
Took me back.
      Whistle it high to the graybeard breakers,
      Where the secret over the great shoal ran.
      Whistle the world that was in my pocket,
      When I had pockets,
      When I was a man.

To a Contemporary Poet

Oh use the simple words
For God's sake, do.
I wade through swamps and jungles
Trying to read you.

Where do you begin
And where do you end?
A simple comma, somewhere
Could be your best friend.

Punctuation, after all,
(Or it seems to me)
Is only a tool, easy to use,
And it comes free.

If sentences butt together
Like cats on a parlor mat,
I struggle to get your meaning
Whether it's this
Or that?

Cold as a Dog

Have pity on your readers
For word gets around. It spreads
That all of us poets
Are a batch of eggheads.

The Lonely of Heart

—W.B. Yeats

On an island a mile or so off the Maine coast, overlooking the sea from a point of rock, is the stone foundation of a house. What must once have been a neat, rather prim fireplace remains intact under the cascaded bricks of the chimney, and a cistern with a brick partition for the storing and filtering of rain water. The house, one can see, was set high—on top of a ledge to begin with. The cellar was made possible only by building up from the rock with big rectangular blocks of stone. Not even the tough skill of Maine workmen could have chiseled a cellar-hole out of the living ledge of red granite.

Some rubbish lies about—not much left now by a generation of souvenir hunters. A dented kitchen pan, bits of thin china, glass oxidized by fire and sun. A kitchen stove lies half-buried in ashes. On the northern wall and creeping slowly along the stones from east to west as the years go by, is a thick woodbine, green in spring and summer, in October a shawl of clear red, bright as courage, against the electric blue of that sea.

Those in the island village who remember when the house was built—my grandfather was one of the workmen—can still repeat some of the terse comments made at the idea of skill and good materials going into it. Granted the summer people were all as crazy as loons and most of them built their houses on the east side of the island to be out from underfoot of the natives, their houses had always been set back at last a little from the shore, among trees. Our own village was on the western shore facing the bay and the quiet beaches, gabled houses sheltered by a shoulder of pasture and thick woods. This "flub-dub" of a house hadn't even a gable to split the wind. It had a mansard roof and a flat expanse of wall reared up to the naked east, as uncompromising as a stubborn woman's chin.

A stubborn woman had it built. She wanted a tough little house and a view of the sea, she said. The workmen grumbled, but when the place was finished it was built to last and as tight as a ship.

"Come a good easterly," my grandfather would say, even years after, "she won't wash off of there, but I wouldn't be s'prised if she had to dump some salt water out of her drawers."

I remember my grandmother giving him a hard look, and my grandfather added, cocking an eyebrow at me, "Bureau drawers, I meant. And while she's hangin' 'em out t'dry, she can look at her view."

Look at her view she certainly could. Her north windows faced three-or-so miles of water and the Mount Desert mountains, the rounded hills set down one after another as in a drawing by a humorous child. To the south were wooded and bare islands, surf-submerged reefs, the rag-tag-and-bobtail of the ending continent. She had the spruces behind her, nudging her tiny lawn, so that when she cut the grass along the edges, she had to lift up their lowest branches, and the mower was clogged with needles. But she had come there for—the North Atlantic, stretching from the ledges outside her window to the sky.

I doubt if she ever knew that because she defied Down East custom, she was never able to live down her reputation among us of being slightly cracked. She would have been distressed, I think, if she had known, for she would have liked to receive the same kindness and respect she gave. But her east windows were always streaked with salt; in a full gale the flowerpots washed off her porch and the sea sent streaming runnels of foam across the lawn, so that the ledge on which the house stood became an island all her own.

Her name was Elizabeth Peterson; she was known in the beginning when she and her mother and friends stayed on the island, only as one of the "Philadelphia ladies."

I don't know what her real background was, but the gossip around the village went that she was a daughter of the owner of Peterson's Magazine, published in Philadelphia in the eighties. Her father was dead, and the magazine, too, and somehow, somewhere, her family had lost a great deal of money. Old Mr. Peterson, the story went on—and heaven only knows where it came from, though it might have had some basis in fact—had had his life insured for thousands of dollars; but on the very day the policy ran out, he died, and his heirs didn't collect a cent. We guessed, however, with wags of the head, that people who could build a summer cottage—local labor, of course, knew how much it cost—and travel back and forth from Philadelphia twice a year, weren't too hard up.

In the early days when a dollar would stretch, Miss Peterson and her mother undoubtedly had a comfortable income, for they hired jobs done about their place and sometimes had a girl in to help around the house. They got my grandfather to build the brick cistern, when, after much digging, it became evident that no well could be had near the house because of the solid ledges. He put in a stone wall, too, to keep the salt spray from ruining the soil of her garden.

Every summer they filled the house with friends, and life must have been comfortable and pleasant in those days before the mother died.

But following the war, during the last part of Miss Peterson's life, her income was smaller than even we on the island cared to think about. We couldn't help knowing what it was, for my father had the general store and post office, and he cashed her checks.

She was a woman about whom much speculation was bound to be carried on. If she had looked like other people she might have shaken down into some kind of accepted familiarity, perhaps have become one of us as the years went by. But she did not look like other people, and she would never shake down into familiarity, facts which she must have known. She was the most calamitously homely person I have ever seen in my life.

The story went—and again I am repeating village gossip—that when she was young, she was beautiful. She had clouds of glossy hair, so said our neighbor who seemed to know, round rosy cheeks, and she was even engaged to be married. But shortly before the wedding—on the day before, in fact, since our neighbor liked her crises clean-cut, as in the case of Mr. Peterson's insurance—she came down with an obscure disease so rare that no other example of it had ever been seen in the "known world."

She was kept out of sight for years, and only shortly before she first came to the island had she begun to appear in public without a veil. The reason she had built her house in such a lonely spot was because she wanted to keep out of the way where she could not often be seen.

So we said. We were then still critical of the house built where the gales could sweep it, and unhappy because we needed a more sensible reason than just that Miss Peterson wished to look at a view.

It seems possible that some calamity of illness had overtaken the poor lady, though it was hard to believe that she had ever been beautiful. Her face was almost literally a death's head, the skin stretched tight, the bones thrusting forward over deeply sunken cheeks, the teeth roundly prominent as in a skull.

We looked at Miss Peterson for the first time, with a sense of disbelief and shock. Then we looked away. But in spite of ourselves our eyes kept stealing back while, painfully, we wished not to look and hoped she did not notice. And never, as long as we knew her—which was for thirty years—did we find out what kind of person she was; not only because she always talked trifles, but because between us and whatever personality she might have kept creeping that wrecked tragedy of a face.

For the rest of her, she was tiny—tinier, perhaps than she looked, for she wore voluminous long black skirts which must have had under them many petticoats; a black jacket over a black, high-necked shirtwaist; an incredible black hat like a stove-lid on her gray, pugged-up hair. Her forehead was wide and intelligent, and she had, I remember, exceedingly clear and piercing eyes, though I cannot remember their color. She talked in a shrill, choppy voice with, of course, a Philadelphia accent, which, in a week's time, every child on the island had learned to mimic.

We were not cruel, I think, for the sake of being so; we must only have been very unsure of ourselves. The island was a mile off the coast and thirty miles from a city. For nine months of the year we saw only each other. We did our shopping for nearly everything but food from the Sears-Roebuck or Montgomery Ward catalogs; occasionally, somebody would get up a "soap order" from the Larkin Company. We were sensitive as only an isolated people can be, suspicious of outlanders—even of the minister and the schoolteacher, who, though they were always people of our own kind from the mainland, were still "from away."

I hope Miss Peterson never knew that we made fun of her behind her back; that we called her "Aunt Pete," and her mother "Our Lady" Peterson; that we said she looked like an old black crow. It was undeniable that she did look a little like one when she went through the village with her long black skirt flopping. If she did know it, she never once in all the years showed that she did.

Her manner to us all, young and old, was always cheerfully friendly. She had trivial conversation for everybody, speaking in her jerky voice about the weather, about the mail being late, about the beauties of nature. And I think there was never a single time when one of us was not polite to her face, answering her trivialities in kind, telling her news of the outside world when we had it, which was seldom in the wintertime.

For she was there in the wintertime after the first few years, she and her mother, and neither of them ever lived anywhere else again.

When the first September came around that they did not close up their house and go away, the village speculated, then wondered. October rolled by, as always a succession of fine days full of thick gold sunshine, as if the sun were swollen with heat that could not reach the earth. The Petersons did not go. Finally, November came, and the first spit of snow.

My father would have died rather than nose into anyone's affairs, particularly one of the summer people. I can remember his throatclearing embarrassment, one day, as he handed Miss Peterson's mail through the wicket and said, "Stayin' late this year, ain't you?"

She looked up from her handful—she always got a lot of mail—with her quick smile. "This is our home now. We're not going away."

I knew my father was flabbergasted, from the way he hesitated. "Won't you be lonesome way off down there?"

"Oh, no, no. I've never been lonesome in my life. And I've plenty to do."

"I guess you will have," said my father bluntly. "Snow gets deep, you know, in them woods."

"Oh, I love the snow and the cold weather. Good day, Mr. Moore. Such lovely weather—this fall sunshine…"

"'t won't last," my father said. But the door was already closing behind her slim straight back. She was quite likely to walk away from you while she was still talking, so that the meaningless sentences seldom came to a full stop, but died away in the distance.

The village was shocked and uneasy, particularly the men. Our Maine men have a very low opinion of the capabilities of women—a fact which always struck me as strange, since they were quite willing to let us lug wood and shovel snow, if we felt inclined, though not to undertake enterprises of our own. The idea of two women—one of them helpless—for "Old Lady"Peterson was eighty and all but deaf and blind—stuck out on that bleak cliff, a mile and a half from a living soul—it wasn't sensible. It wasn't even safe. It was flying in the face of Providence.

How could they keep warm in that fool house, with the temperature twenty below and a gale blowing? They had the same kind of heating we all had—a kitchen cookstove and an airtight in the living room. They also had a fireplace, but the Lord knows, in the wintertime a fireplace is worse than "a hole right out through the side of the house."

Who would lug the wood and coal? Who would lug the water? They had a cistern, but every drop of drinking water had to be carried in buckets from a well five hundred yards from the house.

My mother asked Miss Peterson that question, on the day when she tried, in vain, to persuade her to take a vacant house in the village for the winter.

"Well, I'll tell you," Miss Peterson said. "Lizzie will lug it." She always called herself "Lizzie." When she talked to herself as she often did, she sometimes said, "Lizzie, you old fool."

"Suppose something should happen?" my mother said. "What if you had to have help quick?"

Miss Peterson began to scrabble her things together to go.

"Oh nothing will happen to us." She laughed, her queer half-giggle, half-neigh. "We'll be snug. The worse the storm is the better we like it. We'll take things as they come…" The closing door shut out the sound of her voice.

And so, through the years of my childhood and youth, our wintertimes were accented by the thought of Miss Peterson and her mother, and later Miss Peterson alone, on the shelf of rock, a mile and a half from anybody. It was always good for half-an-hour's conversation on "sewing" afternoon, when women carried on their pastime of gossip known as "havin' it over." We took wind and weather pretty seriously, our menfolk being fishermen. If anyone didn't, we said, it was because she didn't know any better. But as the years went by and we realized the kind of stubbornness she had, our slow reluctant respect for her began to be replaced with admiration.

She tried her best to persuade us not to bother about her. She had a horror of being a nuisance. Often she ploughed through the snow to the village when she didn't need to come for fear we would send someone over to the Head to make sure she was all right. In the winter she came three times a week, on mail day; sometimes more often. She always came, if she could get through the snow, on the day after a heavy storm, that being the time when people were likely to worry.

The worry was legitimate. The road to the Head was little more than a cart-track, studded with root-knobs and stones, and in the dark the section across the Neck was dangerous. The Neck connected the wooded Head with the island proper. It was bare of trees and on its north and south sides thirty-foot banks dropped steeply to rocks and the sea. The path, in those days, ran along the south bank, in some places three or four feet from the edge. In a full gale, the wind made a funnel of that narrow, naked strip of land, sucking across with blasts that could take a man off his feet.

"My God," my grandfather said, "you let a good gust git up under them skirts a hern, she'd go in the air like a balloon."

There were a few occasions when Miss Peterson did not turn up in the village when she was expected. When that happened, two of the men would get into sheepskin coats and rubber boots and go across the island to her house. I can remember my father, tugging on his boots, cursing and swearing, while our husky next-door neighbor, also cursing and swearing, waited for him by the stove. From the remarks they made about those two senseless women, you would have thought they were setting out on a journey to a home for the feebleminded in Iceland.

But they would always tuck her mail carefully in pockets, gather up a gift of fish or lobsters, or a quart of milk; and they never failed to take along snow-shovels.

They would cuss and growl all the way across the island; but, arrived at Miss Peterson's house, they would go up the steps and knock on the door. When she answered, they were ready with a smooth excuse as to why they had come.

"Had to see how many lobster traps washed ashore night, so we brought along your mail," or "Frank and me was lookin' if the snow was too deep to haul wood." No mention of the gifts which were dropped casually on the table as of account; no mention whatever of the real reason for coming. They never knew how she felt about being a bother.

They would then shovel out her path to the well, fill up available buckets and containers with drinking water, bring in coal, heap the woodboxes. When they had done everything they could think of, they would announce that, well, they guessed they'd better be getting along home.

Miss Peterson would say, "Oh. no, no, no, you must come in and have some cake and coffee," and she would set down in easy chairs in her comfortable living room, before crackling open fire, with big plates of devil's food cake and some of the coffee she had hustled to put on when she spotted them coming out into her clearing.

They would sit there, uncomfortable at first, drinking coffee out of the fragile Spode cups, their sheepskins buttoned tightly, their caps on the floor beside their chairs. Then, after a bit, one of them might open his coat and shrug it off his shoulders and stretch out his feet; and the other would follow suit. Bits of village news would pass—whatever there was— nothing much exciting to tell. Miss Peterson would bustle around bringing more cake, filling the cups, putting in a word here and a word there; until, presently, all three of them were laughing and talking ten to a dozen, while the incredibly old and wrinkled lady, Mrs. Peterson, sat rocking in her corner, on her lips her pleasant, uncomprehending smile.

Before they left, Miss Peterson would make her own excuse for why she hadn't come to the village, "I was finishing my rug, and it was so interesting I forgot it was mail-day," or "I was just putting on my galoshes when you came out of the woods." Never a word about the fact that she had got too tired shovel- ing snow, or that she, somehow, didn't feel quite well that day. But I don't think anybody forced anybody.

The men would get up to go, and all the way across the island they would cuss and groan about the bother and the waste of time. They liked it, of course. For after she had lived for a few years among us, we had found out that she loved to entertain; her food was superb; and better than anyone I ever knew she could put people at ease.

I don't know when she started to give her Christmas parties—two each year, one for children, one for grown-ups. I cannot, it seems, remember a Christmas season without them. I must have gone to them from the time my parents considered me old enough to walk to the Head, and back again with the other children at ten o'clock at night. They were lovely parties, of a kind we didn't know—beginning slowly, when we all sat in our best clothes around Miss Peterson's living room, talking in subdued voices and taking surreptitious peeks at her things; building up through games to a sumptuous supper of ice cream and cake, and presents under her Christmas tree. They were never very expensive presents. I remember my disdain one year when I got a pine cone with a red ribbon on it. But it was a very beautiful, symmetrical pine cone, and I wish I had it now. I don't think there was ever a Christmas tree so beautiful as Miss Peterson's. At least I have never seen one, though perhaps I saw it through the eyes of children. Our own trees were trimmed with cranberry and popcorn strings, a little tinsel sometimes, and colored balls when we could get them. Hers had on it every kind of a small bright fragment and miniature toy. I remember some tiny, colored-lace dolls; a doll's trumpet that would blow; some mittens so small that you wondered how anyone could ever have knitted them.

These are the only actual objects I recall. Thinking of that tree now, I see mostly a tall pyramid of glitter reaching to the ceiling, yet I know that there were hundreds of little things on it, and that they were far-off and wonderful and romantic, for they came from places like Germany and Portugal and the Pyrenees. They were things she had collected in the days when she was young and had money and could travel over the world.

It was almost more wonderful that she had cut the tree and set it up and trimmed it herself, and that she had made cake and frozen ice cream for twenty children. But we did not think of that then. We only ate it and afterwards we broke down and had bad manners and did things like dipping napkins into water glasses and throwing them. Miss Peterson never seemed to mind. She played our games with us and seemed to have as good a time as we did. She taught us some new and lovely ones of her own. Those too, I have forgotten. The thing I remember about the games was how, one night, some brat amongst us suggested we play "Ugly Mug."

To this day I don't know whether someone did it on purpose, or whether it was only thought of as a game to play. It wasn't an intelligent game, just something children like when they are excited and don't much care what they play. I have never thought of it since without a kind of creeping horror, though it was not I who suggested it.

You form a ring and say a rhyme which begins innocently enough:

"I put my right foot in (Stamp) I put my right foot out, (Stamp) I give my right foot a shake, shake, shake, And turn my body about."

This you all do, together. The rhyme goes on through several stanzas: "I put my left foot in," "I put my right hand in," and so on, until you have used up your extremities. Then the climax of the frightful thing simply goes:

"I put my Ugly Mug in, I put my Ugly Mug out, I give my Ugly Mug a shake, shake, shake, And turn my body about."

None of us saw it coming. We went through the game with gusto, shouting and stamping the house down, until at the beginning of the last stanza, the thing hit everybody at once. Miss Peterson, of course, was playing the game with us, and she didn't turn a hair when we all stopped as one, and froze into fascinated silence. She merely went on to the end, and we watched her, dumb with embarrassment and shame. She shook, shook, shook her Ugly Mug in and out and finished up with a twirl.

"What's the matter?" she said. "Everybody tired?"

We went on playing something else, but nobody felt much like it, and it was nearly time to go home anyway. So we went. On the way we didn't yell and snowball each other, the way we usually did. The boys didn't run ahead and hide behind trees, so they could jump out and scare the girls. The long shadows the lanterns made on the sparkling snowbanks seemed somehow lonesome, and the woods dark. We just went home and went to bed.

The grown-ups' party was quite a different affair. It was formal—the kind of dinner party, I know now, that Miss Peterson would have given to her Philadelphia friends, had they been within reach. How she could do that and still put at ease those shy and sensitive island people was something to be wondered at. They were of great simplicity among themselves, but to outsiders, complicated; and she was not one of them. But she managed it and they liked it. At least, my mother and father did, I know.

They always went, dressed in their sober best clothes, and I remember well the air of anticipation and festivity—though

it was dignified and somehow solemn—that hung over the
house in the afternoon and early evening before our neighbors
gathered with their lanterns for the walk through the woods.

Miss Peterson would meet them at the door in her best
black dress, usher them in as a well-trained servant would,
to a dressing room to take off their wraps. Then she would
become hostess, gracious and charming, and in no time at
all everybody would be laughing and talking. After a bit, she
would vanish to the kitchen, where as cook and serving maid,
she would talk to herself as she put the finishing touches on
her dinner: "Now, Lizzie, you old fool, you've burnt yourself."

The dinner would be served faultlessly, on the heavy silver
service that had belonged to her family for generations. The
linen was rich and creamy, and under all the graciousness
the fisherman's wives of our village fairly bloomed. They
had white tablecloths at home, for holidays, but nothing like
this! Some of them had old silver—a few thin, worn spoons,
perhaps, brought by their great-grandfathers from England.
But nobody had a plate-rail around the dining-room wall on
which sat old willow plates, fragile and lovely; or a corner
cabinet with shining glass on its shelves.

Seated behind the turkey or chicken at the head of the
table, Miss Peterson would pick up her carving tools and beam
at her guests. "Now," she would say, "which will you have, the
light or the dark?"

I doubt if there was ever a holiday dinner in the village
during those years, at which the father, about to serve the
meat, didn't pick up his fork, and say in a falsetto, imitation
Philadelphia accent, God forgive him, "Which'll you have, the

light or the dark?" But it wasn't all cruel. There was no malice in it, and there was affection behind the laughter.

I used to go to her house often, for as she grew older, she seemed not to mind if children brought the milk and the mail on wet or snowy days. She made us welcome with cake or the baked meringue she called "kisses," and she was always glad to lend the books with which her living room was lined. She had a many-volumed *Nature Encyclopedia,* with lovely colored illustrations, and she tried to get us interested in knowing the names of birds and grasses and mushrooms. There was a book called *The Sea Children,* which I have never seen anywhere else, though I have tried to find it, about a family of fabulous princes with gills, who lived under the sea, rode dolphins and warned against the denizens of the deep. I wish I could remember how many times I borrowed that book. The last time I saw it, its edges were rubbed to fur and every page would come free of its binding.

She herself read what to me were dreadfully dry books— history and travel—but I remember one time I surprised her in the middle of *Tarzan and the Apes.* It was a very remarkable book, she said. Later on, she had a big yellow cat that she actually named "Tarzan."

She loved all birds and animals; they were tame around her house, and she carried on a continual war with boys who hunted in her woods with shotguns. Tarzan, the cat, wore a bell around his neck so that he might never kill birds. I don't think she ever knew that in spite of it he was a mighty hunter.

It was never very much fun to talk to her. She had the same empty conversation for children that she had for grownups. I remember only once seeing below that surface. I had brought over her mail and she looked at the newspaper and saw the headline that Richard Harding Davis was dead. She gave a little cry, and tears came into her eyes. "Oh," she said, "he had been so many places!"

Her clearing was lovely in the summertime, for she planted flowers everywhere. That was not an easy thing to do. The land was mostly solid rock, and every bit of salty earth had to be replaced with growing ground. She did all the work herself, wheeling humus from the swamp and manure from the barnyards across the island, in a tiny wheelbarrow that looking like a child's. Until my grandfather built the stone wall that enclosed her garden, she had to do this every spring, for the sea, in storms, came up across her seedbeds. After many years of slaving, she had flowers growing in every nook and cranny where a root would take hold. You would come up over a shoulder of red granite, close to the sea, and there would be a harebell or so or a sprig of portulaca, sprouting from a crevice in the rock. She planted a hedge of rugosa roses that smelled wonderful in the sea wind. Sometimes on a damp day with an east wind blowing, far back in the woods you could catch a whiff of roses, mixed with spruce and salt.

And every night, through thirty years, she left her lamp burning in her east window until dawn. It was as faithful as a lighthouse, and it became one. The fishermen coming home late at night or before daylight, always took their bearings by it and called it "Miss Peterson's Light."

So there she was, with her kindliness, her eccentric ways that made us laugh, her stubbornness that made us mad. How mad, sometimes, I shouldn't like to say.

There was the time when I met her at the edge of the woods with her lantern. It was early dark, and feeling large and kind toward an old lady, I offered to walk home with her through the woods. I was fourteen that year—an age, I suppose, of benevolence in all young.

She protested firmly, "Oh no, no, no, I have my lantern."

She always said that, as if a lantern were all anyone needed. I think I was probably pretty fulsome in my proposals to go with her, and, at last, we walked along together for a half-mile or so.

It was pleasant, chatting in the lantern light, until all at once I realized how dark it was and how far I was from home. I made some not very graceful excuse, and departed headlong back along the road. The white of the path glimmered faintly, but all around were spruces, big and black, and the bogies rode the back of my neck until, at last, I saw the comforting lights of the village. Just then, out of the corner of my eye, I caught a gleam of light down the path behind me. Half out of my wits with fright, I looked back. It was Miss Peterson with her lantern. She had followed along, to see that I got safely home.

There was also the night of the big storm when she came to the school sociable at the Methodist church. She loved sociables, and I don't think she ever missed one.

It had been snowing early in the evening, but the party went with such bounce and gusto that nobody noticed until we were picking up our things to go home that the whole church was trembling in the gale and that the windows were blocked with snow. Miss Peterson was calmly lighting her lantern when it occurred to the entire village where she had to go to her home.

"Miss Peterson, you can't start out in this! You come straight home with us and spend the night."

They tried all the arguments, but it was evident that, short of force, nothing was going to make her stay in the village.

There was really no need for her to go home: she lived alone now—her mother had been dead for some years.

The men, exasperated, finally gave up. "All right," they told her through clenched teeth. "If you're bound to go, some of us'll have to go with you."

The poor lady—she couldn't have given in to save her life—stood there looking stricken.

"Where's so-and-so? And so-and-so? They better go."

But the two huskiest young men in the village had gone to beau the schoolteacher home. While they were being paged around the church, Miss Peterson slipped out and went on alone.

"Goddam!" said my father. "Ain't got the sense God gave a goose! Come on, Frank, I guess it's up to us."

It was about the worst storm I have ever seen on the coast. We went home single-file, holding to each other's belts. The snow, then, at twelve, must have been three feet deep, with a great cloud of it blasting over the island as if all the mainsprings of the wind had let go. Our house was only a little way from the church, but when we tumbled onto the porch, we had to huddle, winded, for a moment, before we had the strength to open the door into the warm kitchen.

My mother was worried out of her life about my father, but she said very little and got us to bed quickly.

The next morning when I woke up, the room was dark, with only a curious gray light coming from the window. The snow had beaten so hard against the house that it had stuck and crusted there scale-like, a foot thick. I had to chip through with the windowstick before I could break a hole big enough to see out of. The house was like a big lumpy snowbank, with only the chimney showing, and we had seven feet of snow on the level.

My father and Frank had started off through the woods with their lantern, and had got along fairly well until they came to the cleared land on the Neck. There the wind funneled through so hard that they had to get down and crawl. They tried to follow Miss Peterson's tracks, but after a little they couldn't find them. Then the lantern blew out, and they couldn't get it lighted again, so they blundered around, heading into the wind, until they reached the woods on the other side of the Neck. They lit the lantern all right in the shelter of a thicket, but by that time they were lost; so they had to keep going until they reached the shore and could take a bearing. Then they followed the shore until they came to Miss Peterson's house.

The light in her window was burning, and she was sitting by it, tranquilly reading a book.

Going back to the village wasn't so bad, with the wind behind them, but it was three o'clock before my father got home and he was worn out and roaring mad.

"Well," my mother said as he crawled wearily to bed, "I take it she got home all right."

"Yes," my father said. "She did. She flew there. On a broom."

She seemed stranger and more eccentric as she grew older. Perhaps she was. Solitude and loneliness do queer things sometimes. It didn't occur to us that it might have been these which were responsible for her last and most outrageous piece of stubbornness. Her everlastin' pigheadedness, we called it.

The church on the island was Methodist—a small, cold little building, with straight-backed seats and a naked pulpit rearing at the front. The organ was of the pedal variety which laments rather than plays. There we were accustomed to hear, on one Sunday a month, which was as often as the Methodist Conference could spare a minister, sermons of hellfire and brimstone. It was, all in all, a pretty bleak proposition, except I do remember that the bell in the belfry had a singularly sweet mellow tone.

The oldsters in the village were proud of this church, for in their young days they had worked hard to get it. Our grandfathers sometimes took us up into the belfry and showed us the nails that they had hammered with their own hands into the timbers. It seems a pity that their young could not have shared their pride, for their church was a symbol of a fine thing, a kind of unity that held the village together. Perhaps the times were already changing and our religious constitutions were not so tough as theirs. As for me, I know the sermons scared me.

Miss Peterson had always gone to the Methodist church; and so the village was incredulous and mad when she came right out one summer and said her own people had always been Episcopalian. She said she needed something more now than the Methodists had to offer; she said she was going to build an Episcopal chapel.

"Well!" we said to each other. "The Methodist's always been good enough for us" and "What can you expect of them summer people?" (Miss Peterson had then lived among us for twenty years.)

Nobody believed her. We knew that outside of her living expenses she didn't have two cents to rub together. "Aunt Pete's as crazy's a loon," we said. We should have known better.

For two years she scraped and she scrounged. She wrote to Episcopalians in the mainland summer resorts. She talked people into giving a penny here and a dollar there, and somehow, by hook and by crook, she got a Movement started. The wealthy summer people in the resorts, all at once, thought it would be lovely to give a little church to the fisherfolk on the remote island. A neighbor of ours, with his tongue in his cheek, sold Miss Peterson a half-acre of land near the main road in the village. And one summer morning we were thunderstruck when a lumber scow delivered a load at the island and carpenters came to start building.

We were still fairly easy-going about it. Our minister wrote the Episcopalian rector on the mainland and offered him the use of the Methodist church for his services; it seemed a waste, he said, two churches in a town of fifty people. Might not the money be better used for Missions?

The rector wrote back and said, a little coolly, that no, he was sorry, but a place where Episcopal services were held had to be consecrated to them alone. And as for Missions, why, the new church was to be called St. Columba Mission.

And the fat was in the fire.

So our church wasn't good enough for them; so they were so darned holy that they had to be all by themselves. So we were no better than a lot of naked heathens, to be sent a mission to. Well, then, let them build their church and let their so-and-so missionary come. He'd see how many people he had to preach to. Nobody was impolite to Miss Peterson, but some of the elderly people were pretty cool.

We would have been all right if somebody hadn't started the argument as to whether it was idolatrous to get up and kneel down during a service. It stood to reason it was, some said, it was the next thing to the Catholics. Honest wholesome worship was sitting down to a good sermon, maybe standing up once or twice to sing a hymn. All that bobbin' up and down was conspicuous in the sight of God. Church warn't no place t' make a holy show of yourself.

People took sides and tempers rose. The Bible was quoted— "Thou shalt set up no graven images," for such, some contended, the furnishings of an Episcopal altar were. It was surprising that good Methodists should know so much about the Episcopalian service, but many seemed to.

My father said it wasn't as if the Methodists or the Episcopals amounted to a damn as long as it was religion; it was just that we hadn't had a good row for years and were ready for it. But that didn't prevent old friends from passing on the other side of the road with their noses in the air, half for the Methodists and half for the Episcopalians.

The day the new church was consecrated, a crowd of summer people came over from the mainland, and they had three bishops.

"Three bishops!" we said, knowing that the Methodists couldn't have raked up that many to save their lives. "Now ain't that some old holy for you?"

Some of the Methodist faction went to the ceremony out of curiosity. I was dying to go, for it looked pretty colorful, but my grandmother put on her oldest housedress and took me cranberrying. She did, however, peek from the bushes to watch the bishops make a procession down the road in full regalia from the neighbor's house where they had dressed. She sniffed and muttered, "Idolaters!" but I thought they looked lovely.

Miss Peterson was in a seventh heaven for weeks after her church was built. When the novelty wore off and the summer people went away, she had very little congregation. Often, when the rector could get over from the mainland which wasn't often, he and she held services alone. Then, one by one, the children began to go, out of curiosity, and because on the island, there was nothing else to go to.

The little girls, alas, generally appeared without their hats. Their mothers didn't insist on their dressing up for the Episcopal services the way they did for the Methodist. We sneered a little, too, at the seemingly unbreakable rule of the Episcopal Church that ladies couldn't come before the altar without a hat. We wore hats quite automatically to our own services, but we didn't doubt that if we appeared without them, the minister would let us in. The rector, it seemed, wouldn't.

So Miss Peterson kept a box of paper napkins and some pins on a shelf by the chapel door. As each hatless child appeared, she would patiently pin a napkin to the top of her head. I can see now that row of kneeling little girls, with the ruffled paper askew on their bowed heads like so many drunken white butterflies.

After a time, one or two of the children and finally a few younger grown-ups were baptized by the rector, and the Episcopals were in. But the Methodist diehards never forgave Miss Peterson. They said they hoped God would strike them dead if they ever set foot inside her church door. They never did; but God has struck them dead, long since, just the same.

Miss Peterson's church was, in the beginning, quite an ugly little building, rather like a new garage. Inside it was raw with new yellow wood. The day the carpenters moved out, she moved in. She spent her daylight hours planting cuttings from her rose bushes along the foundations, and in front of them bulbs and sets from her own magnificent garden. She wheeled her lawnmower across the island and cut the stiff fieldgrass again and again until the lawn came up fine and green. For three years she worked to make a hooked rug out of silk scraps in tiny delicate loops. It made a rich stream of color up the middle aisle of the church and across in front of the altar. In some curious way it brought mellowness out of the wood and out of the thin, amber-stained glass of the windows. Over the altar she laid lengths of colored cloth embroidered with millions of perfect stitches.

It took her years to finish the church. The new wood darkened in time into a pleasant background. The whole had dignity and quietude, but more than anything else, warmth.

Even now, twenty years after, with the door collapsed on its hinges and the floor rotting away, it is a pleasant place to go. The rug, rainstained, is still on the floor; one of Miss Peterson's priceless embroideries, faded almost white lies across the crumbling altar. Not even the souvenir hunters among the summer people have ever taken any of these things away. The lovely colors are gone, but you can still see the perfection of the work. Spruces have choked out the rosebushes that once grew level with the window sills, and the swallows who live in the rafters make a quiet twittering on a summer afternoon.

Through those years we said Aunt Pete had gone fanatic on religion. Why, we knew for a fact, she spent three-quarters of her time on her knees. At Easter time, so said our neighbor who seemed to know, she fasted and prayed from Good Friday until the next Monday morning. She'd wasted all her money on that church, and the reason she was so thin was because she couldn't afford enough to eat. If that ain't fanatic, went the talk on the sewing afternoons, we didn't know what was.

It is true that during the last years of her life she was very frail and it is true that she was deeply religious. For the rest, she plagues the mind, as those people do about whom nothing personal is known. Without doubt she was lonely, a woman of deep creative passion who needed some of the world's work to do. Perhaps building her church was a last desperate attempt to bridge the gulf between herself and the only human beings she saw from day to day, all other things having failed. I do not know. I think I do know why she lived at the island, away from her kind, alone.

The year I was a junior in college, a friend of Miss Peterson's left her a legacy. It couldn't have been much, but it was enough, she said, to go on a trip. She hadn't been away from the island to stay in twenty-five years, and this was perhaps the last chance she'd get to see the world. She was in her seventies that year—I think, seventy-four. When I went back to school at the end of Christmas vacation, she was on the train.

I had a lower berth, not because I could afford one, but because the train was crowded and I had to take what I could get. I looked for Miss Peterson in the Pullmans, and was puzzled to find that she was not there. It would have been unheard of not to look up a neighbor on the same train, so I walked the length of the cars.

There she was, in a daycoach, sitting straight as an arrow, dressed in the same shabby black clothes and hat she wore on the island, except for a piece of clean yellowed lace at her throat. She was watching through the frosty window the bleak little towns of Maine pull away and be left behind in the dusk and the steam from the engine.

I sat in the seat opposite her for a while, but we didn't talk much. I was wrestling with my soul. I had never had a lower before. A lower was grandeur, and I was not yet nineteen. I think I may have been nicer than I am now, but not so tactful.

"Miss Peterson," I said at last, "couldn't you get a berth?"

She turned from the window with her familiar meaningless smile. "Oh no. I don't need one." But her cheeks flushed thickly, and I saw I shouldn't have mentioned it.

"I mean," I said, making it worse, "the train's jammed with vacation people—I almost didn't get one. What I was going to say was, I'd be glad if you'd take mine. I like to sit up."

"Oh no, no, no. Thank you. So do I."

"Then," I blundered on, blushing to my hair, "wouldn't you please take half of it?"

She simply shook her head and turned back to the window.

I remember thinking with the wrath of the embarrassed young that probably a Philadelphia lady of her generation had never undressed before anybody in her life. It didn't occur to me that for any Maine lady of seventy it would have been quite a departure.

"I'm not going to miss a minute of it," she said, but not to me. She was looking out of the window.

I don't think she realized when I said goodnight. She heard me, because she nodded mechanically. Her eyes were bright and her ugly, unbelievable face was full of suppressed excitement. She didn't seem like someone who had spent years in hiding because she didn't want anyone to look at her. This, now, was what she loved and had longed for—travel in the world, people, things going on. And suddenly I saw that the only home she had was on the island, the only roof left when the others owned by her family were gone. There, only, could she live on her tiny income without asking someone for help.

So much for our neighbor who always seemed to know and for the others who "had it over" on sewing afternoons.

Miss Peterson went to Philadelphia and, after that, Washington. Where else she visited I never knew, except she did get as far as Alaska in the spring. I think I should have gone south, myself, to have sunshine to remember when the bleak Maine winter rolled around again.

She got back to the island in June. I was away working that summer, so that I never saw the picture postcards she brought back of the places she'd been, or heard her tell about her trip to everyone who would listen. It seemed she button-holed people and talked endlessly about it.

"Aunt Pete's hipped on that trip she took," people said, forgetting that last year they'd said she was hipped on religion.

Except for that, she was the same, tending her garden, going to church when the rector came over, very week or so pushing her lawnmower over the church lawn.

The winter that followed was long and cold. In February the island had three feet of snow on the level—deeper in the woods. The temperature went, on some mornings, to twenty below.

There was still talk of "doin' somethin' about Aunt Pete" but the talk was second nature now and nobody really thought seriously of actually getting her to move into the village until spring. She was seventy-five but she wasn't missing trips after the mail.

She came in one bleak afternoon just before dark, and my mother, handling her her letters, noticed that her hands were shaking. "Don't you feel well, Miss Peterson?" she asked, on impulse, knowing quite well what the answer would be.

"Oh yes, thank you," Miss Peterson said. Then, to my mother's surprise, she had hesitated and added, "I'm cold though. I can't seem to get warm." Her tone was thoughtful, my mother said, almost as if she were worried, but in an instant she caught herself up and went on in her usual chatty voice, "I'll go home and shake up my coal stove and have a hot drink."

"Stay and have some supper," my mother said. "Afterwards, one of the boys will walk home with you."

"Oh no, no. Thank you very much," and she scurried up her mail. "It's going to snow, I think, and I…" The closing door hid the rest of it, and my mother saw her go past the window toward the woods, her erect figure in its somber clothes dark against the snow.

The next morning was a little warmer. It had snowed in the night, and when my mother went out to hang her dish-towels on the porch, she saw thick smoke rising over the trees. She thought nothing of it, because the men had been cutting wood in the woodlot the day before, and they had burned brush. It did not occur to her that the brushpile must have been a big one, still to be smoking after all that snow.

At noon, two of the men started out in their boat to go to one of the other islands. As they chugged out past the Head and could see beyond its thick trees, they saw that Miss Peterson's house was gone and that smoke was rising from the place where it had been.

They put back to their mooring and rowed ashore, running white-faced up through the village and stopping at each house on the way. The word traveled fast. Everyone who could walk or who didn't have young children started on the run from wher-ever he was to the Head. It wasn't a question of gathering, for nobody waited. Nobody even stopped to say, "This is what we always said would happen." The whole village just went silently and sick at heart down through the snowy woods.

The foundations of the house were red-hot and filled with blazing embers. The men couldn't tell, but they judged it had burned sometime after midnight, when the village was sound asleep in its snug, western rooms, their windows blinded by frost. Keepers of a lighthouse, far at sea, had seen the blaze at two o'clock, we learned later, and had phoned the mainland.

But on our island, there was no telephone.

No one nearby saw what must have been a scene of mysterious grandeur and indescribable loneliness—the stretch of stormy sea to the east, lighted along its fringes by the flames; the bleak rocks and the laden spruces; the red glare upon the swirling snow.

Around the house the snow had melted, but beyond the heat it was white and unbroken—there were no tracks coming away.

December - 15th

To whom shall I send some Christmas greens?
To the nation's children, short on beans,
With a bottle of ketchup to take the crunch
Out of the cost of a school kid's lunch?

To the U.S. Senators, all good will,
For the state of the budget on Capitol Hill,
Who, hearing the sound of the Christmas bell
Season's greetings, *Joyeux Noel*
Eyed the kitty for means and ways,
And voted themselves a splendid raise?

For any tax payer knows the lift
To a hard-working man of a Christmas gift.

So this I'll send: You've done it again.
God rest you merry, gentlemen.

Remembrance of a
Deserted Coastal Village

The land goes back and it was hard to clear.
Hay-fields, sweat-watered once, are green and lush,
But not with hay—with spruces, everywhere,
With alders and the immortal puckerbrush.

Here once were houses, barns, a pasture gate,
And there the Indians' shell mound, choked with sand.
Five thousand years were not too long to wait
For those who come at last to claim this land.

A little sliver on the end of Time
Unhinged the doors, dropped walls and dried the wells.
The stubborn seeds drove up through lath and lime,
The tough wild roses hid the weathered shells.

Secretly, now, beneath the secret leaves
The essence of forsaken things is blown;
Secret the hanging spider as she weaves,
The golden flies above the cellar stone.

Oh, come away from here for seagulls standing
Stiff-necked and still on their old hip of ledge
Have given us little welcome for our landing,
And he forgets if he be ghost or guest,
Who stays too long upon this echoing edge
Of rock, among the scanty marsh-grass thinning,
To watch the web of water, spinning, spinning,
Past these old ruins, lonely and possessed.

About the Author

Born and raised in the Maine fishing village of Gotts Island, Ruth Moore (1903–1989) emerged as one of the most important Maine authors of the twentieth century, best known for her authentic portrayals of Maine people and her evocative descriptions of the state. In her time, she was favorably compared to Faulkner, Steinbeck, Caldwell and O'Connor. She graduated from Albany State Teacher's College and worked at a variety of jobs in New York, Washington, D.C., and California, including as personal secretary to Mary White Ovington, a founder of the NAACP, and at *Reader's Digest*. Her debut novel in 1943, *The Weir* was hailed by critics and established Moore as novelist, but her second novel, *Spoonhandle* reached great success, spending fourteen weeks on *The New York Times* bestseller list and was made into the movie, *Deep Waters*. The success of *Spoonhandle* provided her with the financial security to build a house in Bass Harbor and spend the rest of her life writing novels in her home state. Ultimately, she wrote 14 novels. Moore and her partner, Eleanor Mayo, travelled extensively, but never again lived outside of Maine. Moore died in Bar Harbor in 1989.